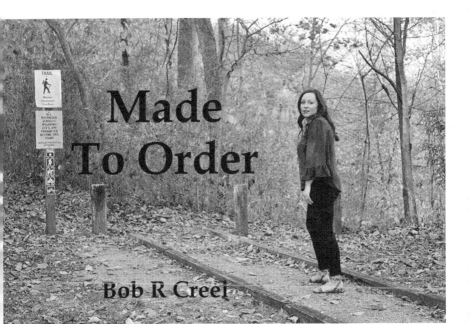

Made To Order

Bob R Creel

WHO DUNNIT

He sits alone in the den of his fine home, Nothing but quiet fills the room,

No noise but the rain falling on the roof;

Suddenly, he hears the phone, this resulted in his impending doom,

The phone rang and poof,

He was dead, murdered by an anonymous caller,

The call triggered a mechanism in the receiver,

A poisonous gas was released, killing the intended victim:

Who did this, was it a man, woman, a person short or taller,

A business partner, jealous lover, wife, not beneath her.

The victim of the crime didn't know what hit him:

Someone who had access, motive, and killer instinct,

Knowledge of his habits, hatred, and contempt,

The suspects are many, but all alibied 'cept a few;

The evidence and motive are outlined and succinct,

The killer performed the task on the first attempt,

Only one person had the opportunity, and utilized what he knew;

Phone tampering, knowing just when to call, hatred, jealousy,;

Pointed to but one person, The Butler, who did it zealously. RDS, SR

The Ripple Effect

Ever throw a rock into a lake or pond and watch what the water does? Yea, the affect I asked about is called the Ripple Effect, and like the rock, a rumor, or a dislike for someone, or a general statement for example about someone can cause a Ripple Effect. This can be done for example in a small town, a large town, a church, a school, a party or gathering, a social media, or especially on mass media, where everything is taken as truth. The harm, caused by the Ripple Effect, on a person's reputation cannot be measured and can affect almost anyone or everyone, as the case may be. Now, some people are thick-skinned, and the Ripple Effect won't bother them, but in so many cases, this can destroy people by reputation or emotionally, some slightly and some extremely. Now, this can be a very useful weapon, you may think, if you're that type of person who likes to belittle and ruin others, but let me warn you. "Let he that is perfect cast the first stone" from a quote from the Bible by Jesus, because that ripple caused by the stone could come back and hurt you otherwise.

Bob R Creel

Preface:

I'm a novice, and at times when writing a creative fiction novel, which, this is pure fiction by the way, you get the feeling you're in over your head, and sometimes you feel this more than once. I've spent years writing this in bits and pieces of when I could get a little time to devote to it. You see I held two jobs and helped raise a family, while I was writing, otherwise, this book would have possibly been on the shelves earlier.

Table of Contents

CHAPTER 1
Starting Over

She moved from socially, elite surroundings to a place that was very common, simple to say the least. This place she had moved to was plain and unassuming. She was distressed and dismayed at the thought of possibly being here the rest of her life. She was accustomed to a life with a higher standard of living, and now, she must live in a one bedroom apartment on money allocated to her by the court system. After a lengthy divorce, her monies had been slowly dwindling away. When the decree was in that she would only receive a monthly expenditure check, which was far less than she was used to, her dreams and fantasies of having a healthy settlement to rely on disappeared. Having only the best and all the money she needed, the social balls, the bridge parties, the lounging beside the pool, were all a thing of the past and now the girl was alone and distraught.

The girl, Kara, lost her divorce case because of one single reason. The judge was a woman, who sympathized with her husband, because he had been beaten severely by Kara's lover in a fight. Yes, she caused the marriage to break up, but she wasn't totally to blame because she was raised believing anything she saw and wanted, she could get, and thus was the case with the men in her life.

As she walked into her new apartment, which was anything but new, she sighed with disgust at the size and abhorrent living conditions, so drastically different than what she was accustomed to. The first thing to do was to clean her new abode, which didn't appear to have been touched in quite a while, and then she must find a newspaper in order to search through the help wanted ads. Money would have to be earned to supplement her meager check. Little did she know, that though her life had already changed, the biggest change was yet to come.

Kara had come to many resolutions concerning her current situation. She had sworn not to make the same mistakes as before. Now, she would not be involved with men, and the lifestyle she had known would be put behind her. This was the reason she had moved to this obscure little town, Rossville, more than 200 miles from her previous home where her troubles all began. Kara still had her looks and a certificate as a teacher. She would get by.

The next day brought rain and warm temperatures for April, as Kara ventured forth to start her new life in the small mid-western town. Her first stop was the elementary school, where she submitted an application to substitute teach. Next stop was the high school, where she applied for English teacher. Kara was still not enthusiastic about her interviews, so as another attempt at something in her field, she visited the public library. Upon arrival, she was immediately greeted by an elderly lady with a cheerful smile, who asked, "Can I help you?" Kara replied,

"I'm new in town and I've come about a possible position. Could you please direct me to a supervisor in charge of hiring?" The elderly lady pointed to an office near the stairway on the second floor and said, " Mr. Reeves is who you would want to talk to." and then turned and began to walk away. Kara climbed the stairs and turned toward the office nearest to the stairs and knocked on the door facing, as the door was already open. From inside came a solemn voice, "Come in. What can I do for you?" Then Kara, a little intimidated, replied, "I, uh, well I'm new in town and I need work. I was wondering if you might have something for me at the Library." The man, a middle aged, distinguished, and handsome man, stood up, and immediately said, " Come in and have a seat." He continued, "My name is Matt Reeves and I'm administrator for the Library. And your name is?" Kara, with more confidence, stated," My name is Kara Steele, how do you do?" "Very well, thank you" replied Matt "And, I suppose I can tell you that we will be needing someone to help Ms. Abbott, who is getting up in age and needs assistance with the Library procedures." Kara couldn't help but beam a little, since this sounded very promising. She and Matt talked a while about the duties in the library and the education needed to comprehend the system used in the library. Other conversation included experience and desired salary, which both agreed upon. Since, the noon hour was approaching, Matt asked Kara," How about if we discuss all of this over some lunch?" Kara agreed and they both got up to leave.

At lunch, Kara manipulated the conversation, so as not to have to answer very many questions about her past. But questions did arise. For instance, Matt, while eating, asked "Have you been divorced long?" then Kara, with a puzzled look, replied "How did you know I was divorced?" Smiling, Matt answered, "Someone as pretty as you is either married or divorced, and since you aren't wearing a wedding ring, you must be divorced." Becoming evasive, Kara stated abruptly, "Not for long, but what about you? Have you lived here long?" Matt responded with," I have been living here since graduated from college, about seven years, and I have been married ten years to the same woman and have two children." Kara nodded and changed the subject, so as to stay away from questions of her past. She asked Matt, "What do people do for entertainment in town?" and Matt replied "Oh, they usually go out to dinner, or see a movie, or if you wanted something more exciting you would have to go to nearby Chaffee, a town of approximately 30,000 people, located about 20 miles west of Rossville." He continued, "Chaffee offers the most recreation for 100 miles," The lunch ended with Matt shaking Kara's hand and saying how pleased he was to meet her and that he would be in touch. The lunch date left no guarantee for Kara that she had the job.

Later, she decided to see the town. Main Street was lined with local businesses from a hardware store to some jewelry stores to even a book store, and as was to be expected, the businesses were like the town-quaint and very simple. To pass some time, Kara began to window shop and investigate the row of shops, when she came upon a combination deli and pizza restaurant and decided to stop in for a soft drink before continuing. As she sipped her drink, three ladies of retirement age came into the restaurant and began to sit in the booth next to her. Kara could hear their conversation, which had now turned to gossip. She paid little attention to the conversation, until she overheard one of the ladies say, "I heard that nice Matt Reeves and his wife are having problems." " It seems his wife is having mysterious rendezvous with the new guy in town." One of the other ladies spoke up, "You don't mean the Real Estate Broker who just opened a business in town?" and before the first lady could reply, the third lady exclaimed, " My word!" and they all leaned back in their seats. One of the ladies went on to say, " His name is Bruce Stanton, and ever since he moved here six months ago, he has become the most eligible bachelor in town." Another lady chimed in, " He moved here from Chaffee, and he drives a new Corvette convertible." " How old is he? " one of them asked and got an instant response " Thirty, I think." Kara had learned all this in a brief fifteen minutes, but now the topic of discussion had changed to the town doctor's new nurse, and Kara was ready to leave now. Kara left the restaurant and ambled homeward, where she entered her apartment and immediately fell on the bed, weary from the day's activity.

When she awoke, Kara saw that it was nearly nine o'clock and realized she hadn't eaten since lunch. She brushed through her long auburn hair and put on some make-up and eased out the door and proceeded directly back to the deli she had been to earlier. Once there, she ordered and had a seat in the same booth she was in earlier so as to wait for her food.

While waiting, Kara noticed that the people operating the deli were different than the others she had seen earlier. The people now were a handsome couple in their late twenties, probably man and wife, she thought to herself. The man had sandy, brown hair and a mustache and was of average build, while the lady had soft, brown hair and hazel eyes. Kara thought how handsome the man was, and immediately dismissed the thought, since he was obviously married to the lady beside him. With the arrival of her food, she began eating and noticed a petite, blonde haired woman, approximately her own age, staring at her from across the room. With a smile, Kara waved at the girl, and continued eating. At that moment, the blonde started across the room toward Kara's table and smiling, said, "My name is Linda Kaplan, and I noticed you're alone. You're new in town aren't you?" Kara stopped eating and replied, " Yes, I am. I just arrived in Rossville and I am alone." " My name is Kara Steele and I've only met a few people so far. It's nice to meet you." Then Linda asked, "Are you planning on staying? Where are you from originally?" Kara didn't especially want to talk about her past and in an attempt to avoid any more personal questions about her past, she simply stated, " I'm from a city many miles from here called New Wales. Have you heard of it? "And paused and continued "But let's talk about Rossville. Are there any dark secrets about the town that I should know about?" Linda replied "No" with a smile and then resumed, saying "Only the local gossip is all. "

The two women talked, a while, mostly about the other women in town and of course the eligible men Rossville had to offer. This subject caused Kara to lose interest in the discussion, because at this time, Kara had heard all she wanted to hear regarding men. Kara excused herself, and finished eating. Then Kara made her way homeward, toward her small apartment, noticing the quaintness of the small town she had moved to, the small shops and the cobblestone streets of downtown offered much appeal, she thought.

Upon arriving at her apartment, Kara found Matt waiting for her at her front door. Without pausing, she asked Matt, " Can I help you?" and proceeded to place the key in the door. Matt cleared his throat a little and proceeded to tell Kara that he was passing by and thought he would stop by. Kara looked at him and said, " You were not really just passing by, so I'll ask again, what can I do for you? As she entered the doorway. By this time Matt had gained some composure and stated, "There is something I need to talk to you about, and I couldn't say anything earlier." Kara could tell Matt had had a few drinks and started to simply tell him to talk to her another time, when she thought that this could be her future employer and she didn't want to get off on a bad start. She asked, "Would you like to come in?" Matt shrugged and began to say, "I can't stay long, but I really need to talk with you. Maybe we could meet for dinner tomorrow evening, if that's ok with you?" Kara thought a minuteand sheepishly nodded a yes. "Tomorrow at 6:30 at Mitchell's then." Matt said and turned to leave. Mitchell's Restaurant was one of the nicer restaurants in town and offered private seating.

The more Kara thought about the situation and the date she had just made, she became hesitant about the whole thing. Here she had decided to stay away from men, since her divorce, and now, she was about to get into, well she didn't know what she was getting into. She only knew that she did not want to make the same mistakes she had made in the past. She decided that she would hear him out and try to dodge any kind of relationship other than employer/employee, and with that she laid on the bed and fell off to sleep while listening to the rain on the roof, as it had just begun to rain.

The next day, Kara awoke to sunshine pouring in through the window. She rose to draw the curtains And began to prepare herself for the day, the thoughts returned. What if he were attracted to her. After all, this was what she had tried to get away from by moving to Rossville. No matter what his reasons, she must end it before it starts. She continued to get ready for the date.

Matt was waiting for her at the rendezvous point as Kara entered the local restaurant with prying eyes turned toward her and her date. As she sat down, she couldn't help but blurt out without really thinking. "Now look!" and before she could finish, her eyes caught the look of dismay on Matt's face and she hesitated. "I had to talk to someone" he said, "and you're the logical choice, being new in town. " He went on to explain, "You see, my wife's family is very well known here and everyone in this town is connected with them in some way or another, and so I couldn't very well talk to anyone or else it would get back to my wife." After hearing this, Kara took pity on him and decided to hear him out. At that moment, the waiter came by to take their order and bring them water to sip on while waiting. After ordering, they saw the waiter leave, "What else?" she asked in a demanding tone. Matt paused and stated " Maybe, this isn't such a good idea, after all." But, Kara apologized and insisted he continue. Matt took a sip of water and began to tell her the reason he had brought her here. "My wife has done this before, and each time she denies it. If not for the children, I would have gone a long time ago, but now it's too late for that. So, what I'm asking of you, is that you be seen with me at several places to allow my wife to become jealous and in this manner, we could give our marriage another chance." With this, Kara slumped in her seat.

"What makes you think it will work?" she asked.

"I have to do something," he replied.

Kara thought how much she had been like his wife during her marriage and wandered if a scheme such as this would have changed things in her own previous marriage. She also knew by the outcome of her divorce that ending a marriage is harmful to everyone involved and there were children to consider in this case. "I'll do it on one condition and that is my getting employment at the Library will not be affected," she stated. Matt agreed and said this would not affect her employment, since after all it was innocent in every way.

The next few days were uneventful for Kara. She went out occasionally, only to find the town to be sort of dull and boring. After all, she hadn't met anyone new and didn't know the people she had met well enough to call them. Kara came to the conclusion that she was in the wrong place. Then on the evening of the tenth day in Rossville, she received a call. It was Matt and he wanted to make a date for the following day, Saturday, at seven o'clock for dinner. She hesitated, but remembered what had transpired a few days ago and agreed to meet him.

The next evening at Maurice's, a semi-nice, eating establishment, Matt was waiting patiently for Kara's arrival, when he saw her enter in a gown that turned all eyes toward her. After all she was an attractive woman with a good figure and nice features. They greeted each other and began discussing the arrangement they had made. But before Kara could say anything, Matt interrupted and declared "You got the job." Kara paused and questioned, "You?" Matt smiled and proceeded to tell her the board of directors had to okay new employees, "but" he stated, "I did put in a good word for you."

The conversation went on about her new duties and title and then they were approached by the waitress. After ordering, the two decided to have a drink, so Matt nodded at the waitress to get her attention and they ordered their drinks. In the time that followed, probably 20 to 30 minutes, they talked about Matt's problems. When the food arrived, they were sullen and Wrapped up in the conversation, which had changed as soon as the waitress arrived on the scene. During the meal and immediately afterwards, the talk was of the town and parties held by the socialites of Rossville. After eating, Matt and Kara had a few drinks and chatted. No one counted, but both were feeling pretty good as time progressed to 10:30 p.m. "I think it's time to leave" Kara spoke with a slurred speech. While leaving, Matt wanted them to walk a little slower, so more people would see him with Kara, and thus his wife would learn of it. They continued to walk and ended up at Kara's apartment building. Matt walked her upstairs, but as he got closer to the entry, Kara stopped him abruptly at the door and said "That's not part of the deal." He threw his hands in the air, shrugged, and said "All right" and kissed her on the cheek and started walking away, saying "See you Monday, 8:00."

Monday morning at 8:00 sharp, Kara waited on the Library steps for the doors to open and at that time, the door swung open to reveal Matt with a set of keys. He motioned her to come in and started telling her of what her duties consisted of; in a professional, businesslike manner. Her title would be Research Director, and she would be in charge of researching, censoring, and procuring new books and magazines for use in the Library. This seems cushy, but the number of books and magazines coming into the Library was estimated at one hundred to one hundred fifty every six months, which meant an awful lot of reading for someone, and Kara was only allowed one assistant to help her. Her work was truly cut out for her, and Kara realized this by the end of the day, as she sorted through order forms and stock summaries until 5:00 pm, while skipping lunch. At home, she prepared a sandwich and a glass of milk, ate and dozed off from exhaustion.

A few weeks went by, and Kara was getting accustomed to the work, so the job became easier. Matt had tried to initiate some dates, but she was able to put him off due to the workload. Now, he was asking, again, to meet her at a little bar around the corner from the Library after work, and she finally agreed, since this was the fourth time he had asked her. She was still afraid of getting into a relationship. She had only agreed to meet him in the first place because he said it was to make his wife jealous, so his kids would not be devastated by divorce. At Kaleb's Place, the bar Matt had spoken of, as they sipped their drinks, Kara uttered forth "This is the last time." Matt looked at her and knew what she meant, but asked, "What do you mean?" and she went on "Your wife should have gotten word by now and remember the idea was to make her jealous." Matt then explained, "She has asked about another woman and she has been more attentive toward me, but I'm not certain if she is ready to give up… well you know, her other activities." This was Kara's boss talking as if he wants to continue the arrangement, but she was wanting to end it." How do I get into these situations?" She said to herself. She decided to try a different approach and ordered another drink. The evening went on, and they were here two and a half hours more and ordered one drink after another, while talking, drinking, and laughing.

Upon leaving, Kara asked Matt to walk her home and at her apartment door, she asked him to come in for a few minutes. Once inside, Kara decided to take the aggressive to see what would happen. After all, Matt was handsome, and it would be to end their relationship, not to start one. She thought by taking the aggressive, the worst that could happen is the two would do what was slowly happening anyhow. Kara moved toward Matt and began to undo his shirt, teasing with her fingers as she moved from one button to the next. Matt was becoming a little flustered at this and asked, "Are you sure you know what you're doing?" As she pulled the shirt back to take it off, Kara spoke softly saying, "This is what you really wanted, isn't it?" With that she pulled the shirt off and flung it to the floor. Next, her fingers went to his belt buckle and began working with it. Matt sighed, "Maybe, this isn't such a good idea." He continued, "I want my wife to think I'm having an affair to make her jealous. I'm not wanting to really have an affair." Kara smiled and said, "Then we might as well stop right here with our agreement, because, this is what it's leading to." Matt nodded so as to agree and began putting his clothes back on. "Just a minute," he began, "would you have gone through with it if I were willing?" Kara put her hands back on his belt buckle and asked, "What do you think?" Matt smiled and started out the door.

The next couple of days at work were trying for both Kara and Matt. Finally, Matt suggested they still be friends and have an occasional lunch together, and Kara agreed.

The following weekend found Kara at the deli again, and there also, was Linda Kaplan, who Kara had met when she first moved to Rossville. Linda motioned for her to join her table where two other women were enjoying a soda. Kara, reluctant, strolled over to the table where she had been invited to sit and thus began the introductions. Linda introduced Kara as the new girl in town and introduced the two women as friends, Sandra Trask and Louise Jinny. Sandra was a small woman of about thirty two with brown hair and brown eyes, while Louise was about twenty seven and had red hair and blue eyes, also small framed. After sitting, Kara learned that Sandra was married, but Louise wasn't and tonight was the girls' night out. Their talk shifted back and forth as to where to go and what to do, and then Linda asked Kara to join them. Her reply was not immediate, but she did not have anything else to do, so why not. As the four got up to leave, Linda, voiced "Pick you up at seven" and everyone nodded in assurance. The night on the town with the girls proved to be entertaining for Kara. They traveled to Nearby Chaffee and spent time at several of the town's nightspots. Mostly gossip and polite compliments were all that were exchanged during the night between the four women. The greatest amount of talk was devoted to one person, a Bruce Stanton. It seems the ladies really got great pleasure from talking and fantasizing about the sexy and eligible bachelor with with his new sports car and debonair appearance. The two married ladies proclaimed that he was most certainly in their dreams, while the two single women, Louise and Kara, agreed that no man deserved that much attention, even if he was good looking.

The girls drank and talked into the night, and finally decided it was time to start homeward. On their way out of the city, one of the women spoke up and said, "Look over there. I believe That's Bruce's car parked in front of that bar." At this point, they were all a little tipsy, but it was Sandra, one of the married in the group, who exclaimed, "Stop the car!" And Linda, smiling a big grin, immediately found a parking spot. They filed out of the car a little awkwardly and headed for the door to the bar with Sandra in the lead. Once inside, their eyes searched for Bruce's blonde hair, until Linda, who remained to be the most sober, pointed to a table in the center of the room where Bruce and another man and a woman were seated. The four sat at a table nearest Bruce's table and ordered more drinks. After some discussion as to whether they should interrupt, Sandra, now very tipsy, asserted with great zeal, "Yes". With this, she rose from her chair and stepped over to Bruce and said "Excuse me, but aren't you from Rossville?" Introductions commenced, Sandra introduced herself and proceeded to introduce Linda, then

Louise, and as Kara was introduced, she said "Hi" and kept on drinking. Bruce asked her, "You're not from Rossville, are you?"

"Just moved there" she replied.

Sandra, by this time was feeling a little hurt, since after all, she was the one who initiated the conversation with Bruce. She started toward her seat, sat down and began sipping her drink. Bruce, recognizing the hurt, turned his attention toward Sandra, saying "What are you ladies doing tonight? Are you out on the town?" Then Sandra felt recognition and began smiling. Kara liked this and looked at Bruce, a look of approval.

The next hour was spent drinking and talking with occasional glances directed toward Bruce by all the women. It seemed to Kara, that all this attention might affect Bruce's ego, but he continued to talk to the girls as if they were old friends until he stated "Why not have a party at my place next weekend and you're all invited and bring a friend or spouse." Then he turned to Kara and asked "Are any of you married?" Kara replied, "Two of us are married and two of us are not." And with that declared, "Shouldn't we start home? It's getting pretty late."

The next week was uneventful for Kara and work seemed to be so slow, so she was actually looking forward to the weekend. Bruce's invitation to party looked better to her every day. By Thursday, she had decided that she would go to the party, and she would also buy something new to wear. Rossville didn't offer much, but there was one store named Claire's which caught her attention. The apparel, there, was appealing and the prices were affordable. When she entered, to her amazement, she saw two of the women she had been with the previous weekend, Sandra and Louise.

"Shopping for the party?" Louise asked.

"I thought I might as well buy something new. How about you?" Kara replied. The ladies talked awhile, said some farewells, and resumed shopping.

That Saturday night came quickly and Kara was enthusiastic about the party, now. She had a new outfit, a new job, and a new outlook on things in general, including men. When she arrived at the party, she gazed adoringly at Bruce's home, an old Victorian style house, like something from a magazine on beautiful older homes. Since he was in Real Estate, she supposed it was easy for him find this grand old home. Kara was greeted at the door by Bruce, who appeared very glad to see her saying, "I'm very happy you could come. Have any trouble finding the place?"

"No, none at all, and by the way, you have a lovely home," she replied as the two started down the hall together. At the end of the hall was a spacious living room and Kara thought that half the town must be here. Once inside, she could recognize some people by name, but most she recognized by face only. Bruce immediately began introducing her to everyone and when this was done, he asked, "Can I get you something?" and left to retrieve a some drinks.

While waiting for Bruce to return with the drinks, Kara noticed Matt in the crowd standing beside a pretty, petite woman with short brown hair, and she knew instantly that this must be his wife, whom Kara had never met, but had heard so much about. As she looked on, Matt glanced her way and immediately excused himself to the people he was talking to, and he and his wife proceeded toward Kara. When Matt and his wife reached her, he said with a certain exuberance, "Kara, this is my wife, Beth. Beth, this is Kara, who I told you about." Beth responded with, "You didn't tell me how pretty she was though," and smiled. Pleasantries were exchanged between the two, both unknowing what the other had heard from people, including Matt. This made it awkward and left each with a certain air of distaste for one another. As Beth saw Bruce approaching with the drinks, she excused herself and began to mingle with the other guests in an effort to avoid Bruce. It was evident also, that Matt had some feelings toward Bruce, as he also left saying, "I believe I'll join my wife; see you later." Bruce handed the drink to Kara and asked, "Are you having fun?" Kara nodded as she proceeded to look out over the crowd of people of which she estimated to be around forty to fifty in number. She made a motion in the direction of a couple and asked "Who is that couple? I recognize them from the bar I visited in Chaffee." Bruce glanced toward the couple and explained, "They're friends of Matt Reeves and his wife, Beth. I really don't know them that well." She then pointed out a few more couples, which she had noticed and Bruce replied, "They are some of the prominent figures in Rossville and most of the people here are from Rossville." He then asked Kara, "Do you want to meet some of these people? Come on," Bruce said, "let me introduce you." And so, they began mingling and meeting the guests, while drinking, laughing, and observing a few sexual gestures, such as looks and raised eyebrows, from the men and some disapproving looks given by the females in the group. After all, Kara, with her beauty intact, is a most appealing woman and is bound to get looks, since she is also the new girl in town and thus receives a lot of attention due to this. As the party progressed through the night into the wee hours of the next morning, virtually everyone was either considerably intoxicated or on their way to being there, when suddenly, the noise of the party was interrupted by screaming and shouting coming from the entry foyer. "The Reeves are at it again." Stated someone standing near Kara. She was moving her head back and forth as to see where the shouting was coming from, when she decided to move closer to the ruckus till she was finally standing at the door to the foyer. Beth Reeves was swinging her purse and cursing at her husband. From what Kara could gather, Beth was accused of flirting with one of the guests, a Mitchell Blake. While being accused of having her hand on his leg, she went into a frenzy and began to storm out the door. As she was leaving, Matt screamed at her, "We're finished, you've embarrassed me for the last time, don't ever show your face around me again, or I'll ....." he paused, bowed his head, and made his way outside. Kara saw his despair and went outside to possibly comfort him for now she could see how her own marriage had affected her ex-husband. "Matt, I'm sorry," said Kara.

"Don't be sorry. It's not your fault. Just go away!" Matt exclaimed. She could see that he needed to be alone and turned to go back inside.

Kara re-entered the party, which by now was doomed to disband within the next hour. She spoke with Bruce saying, "That was terrible. I feel so sorry for Matt." Bruce replied, "I know, Matt is a nice guy and his wife is a notorious flirt, and she has been out with other men making her every move suspicious."

"I'm ready to leave after that. I'll see you later," said Kara.

CHAPTER 2

The Blame Game

The following day was Sunday, and Kara had no plans for the day, so she decided to visit the pizza parlor and see if there was any gossip on the previous night's happenings. And besides, it was getting close to lunch, and she hadn't eaten yet. Upon arrival, she sat at the table nearest the door and ordered a cup of coffee. Sipping her coffee, she noticed a couple of women who were across the room from her, glancing at her and talking amongst themselves. Kara dismissed this as the usual gossip and continued to drink her coffee. She then ordered a slice of pizza and again looked at the women across from her, and found that they were no longer looking her way, and this made her feel relieved. Little did she know, that their gossip was just the beginning of her involvement in something which would bring great changes to Kara's life.

As Kara left the restaurant, Bruce eased up beside her in his maroon Corvette and rolled his window down and asked, "Care for a ride?" Kara smiled and accepted demurely. It had been a while since she had ridden in a sports car and now this was fun. The two talked "You're out pretty early considering when the party ended last night, aren't you?" Bruce asked. Kara looked at him and replied "Oh, I don't know. It really wasn't that late, last night," she went on to say "You know, I had a couple of dates with Matt, purely platonic, you understand." Bruce listened intently and said "I know you were seen with Matt a couple of times in different places, but you work with him, don't you? And that's nobody's business but yours and his in my book." Kara, feeling good about the conversation so far, spoke out, "We had an arrangement." "I didn't want you to get the wrong idea." She continued to say.

They rode around for a period of time, talking and getting to know each other. They were both relatively new to the community, Kara being the newest resident of the town, and this was good to talk about, because they could compare thoughts about the people and town. Later, it was Kara, who said, "I believe it's time for me to get home and rest. Tomorrow is a work day and I'm anxious to talk to Matt again about his problem." Bruce turned the car toward Kara's apartment and offered to walk her upstairs. At the door, he said his farewells and left, saying, "I will be seeing you again. You can count on it. And if you need anything, just yell." Kara felt that this could be the beginning of something, and for the first time in a long time, she was favorable of, maybe, getting into another relationship with a man.

Kara then laid her purse on the end table and started for the bedroom to lie down for a nap. She had been napping for about thirty minutes, when there came a knock at the door. She got up, straightened her hair and washed her face, so as to wake up and proceeded to the door. When she opened the door, there appeared two police officers. "Are you Kara Steele?" one of the officers questioned. Kara replied, "Yes, I am. What seems to be the problem?" Then the other officer said, "Could you please come with us? Our chief would like to talk with you." Puzzled and bewildered, Kara agreed to come along and reached for her purse as she was escorted through the door and down the hall to the stairway. Once she was in the police car, Kara asked, "What's this all about, anyhow?" There was no reply, only silence from the two policemen. The station was only a half mile from her apartment, and upon arriving, she was brought before the chief of police, a burly man of about 6 feet and two hundred fifty pounds with dark features, dark hair, and a grim look on his face. "Now, will you tell me why I'm here?" Kara blurted out. The curiosity and her outrage at being brought here with no explanation was about to get the best of her. He replied, "Sit down. Can I get you anything?" Kara shook her head as to say no, and he continued, "What do you know about the Reeves, Ms. Steele, that is your name, is it not?" Kara thought for a moment. "So, that is what this is all about," she thought. They must have had another fight, and Beth filed a complaint. Now, Kara responded, "Yes, that is my name, but I only moved to Rossville recently and I do work for Mr. Reeves at the library." The chief looked at her and said with a stern voice, "You have been seen around town with Mr. Reeves both day and night. And you must know he is a married man, do you not?" Kara quickly replied, "I can explain that. You see, Mr. Reeves asked me to do him a favor by meeting him in different places, so as to make his wife jealous, you see. He said his marriage was shaky, and he thought that would be the way of saving their marriage." The chief stood up and turned his back to Kara and said, "Uh-huh, I believe you were having an affair with Matt Reeves and his wife would not give him a divorce, and so, either you or both you and Matt Reeves plotted to kill Beth Reeves, and now she's dead," he said forcefully. Kara's eyes became big and dilated as she let out a moan of surprise and disbelief. "How did it happen?" She asked. "You're saying you have no knowledge of Mrs. Reeves' death, Ms. Steele?" Asked the chief. "We know why you killed her, but we, as of yet, don't know the details of how and when or to be more precise, the exact time you killed her. But, I guarantee that when we do, we'll be looking you up Ms. Steele. Right now, you are our best suspect, so don't be leaving town on any extended trips until we get to the bottom of this," he pronounced. "That's all for now!" The chief exclaimed and turned to look away from Kara as to dismiss her. Kara raised up from his desk and exited the room. The chief turned to one of his officers and stated "Take her back to her apartment and don't say anything to her, but keep an eye on her and follow her. I want to know where she goes, who she meets, and anything she does. And don't let her know you're following her or anyone she sees," he added. The officer led Kara to his car and began to drive her home, when he noticed a tear starting to run down Kara's cheek.

As the police car, that dropped Kara off, sped off, another unmarked police car is in position down the street, just watching. Then as Kara was just about to enter her apartment building, she noticed Bruce's car turning the corner toward her and she stopped before entering. Bruce pulled up to the curve and got out to greet Kara, who was now showing signs of anticipation and immediately asked "Bruce, do you know what's going on?" Bruce looked at Kara and with a sigh, begins explaining, "They found Beth Reeve's body this morning at Circle Park and they have been questioning anyone and everyone who might know anything about her death." Kara replied, "Yes, I just came from the police station where they interrogated me and accused me and Matt of plotting her murder. The chief said he didn't know the how, when, and where it happened as of yet, but he said he had some ideas." She added, "He thinks Matt and I are lovers, because we've been seen together a few times." Bruce interjected with, " I wouldn't worry too much. He's grasping at straws." Kara paused to gather her thoughts and exclaimed, "Bruce, you have to help me. Those rendezvous with Matt to make his wife jealous now look suspicious and being new in town, and not having an alibi for after the party, I could be charged with murder!"

Bruce reached for Kara's hand to console her and said, "Why don't we get a cup of coffee and mull over this situation, because as you know, I could become under suspicion too." At the café, they sipped coffee and reflected on the party of the night before. They both agreed that the fight between Beth and Matt would place Matt under suspicion. Not only was he the husband, but the fight they had was witnessed by many people. And, since Kara had been seen with Matt at several times, she could see how the chief could suspect her as well. Kara and Bruce continued to talk over the state of affairs, but neither could arrive at a solution to the predicament that was facing them.

Bruce paid for the coffee and agreed to walk with Kara to relieve some tension.

They walked down Main Street passing the shops and stores, talking as they went. Suddenly, Kara blurts out something, that she was reluctant to say, but had heard the ladies at the Deli say earlier, "Bruce, you had an affair with Beth, didn't you? At least that is what I've heard." Bruce replied coyly, "There was nothing to it, Kara. Beth pursued me for a while, but when I didn't return her attention, she stopped. Still, there were rumors about you two and since you are sort of new here too, they could suspect you as well," Kara states.

Bruce replied, "I don't believe I'll be a suspect, but it is possible." She went on to say, "Wouldn't it be better if we two worked together to, well, clear our names?" Bruce stared into a store window, looking kind of distant and replied, "I don't advise doing anything on your own, but if you learn something useful, we can take it to the police together, and if you need anything, you know I'll help in any way I can."

That night was spent by Kara considering her situation. The facts were obvious, a woman was murdered, Kara was a suspect due to her acquaintance with the victim's husband, and since she was new in the community, no one would believe her innocence. And with her past experiences with men, Kara would have a hard time explaining her way out of this quandary. The police has already decided she was a guilty party. So, she decided she would have to look into the matter on her own, since she couldn't afford to hire an investigator. But, she thought out loud, "Where will I begin?" She then decided to go to bed and hope to get some sleep.

The following morning, Kara was refreshed and, after some intense thought, knew where she must start. After her second cup of coffee, she picked up the phone and dialed Matt Reeve's phone number. A woman answered at the other end of the line, and said, in a remorse tone of voice, "Hello, you've reached the Reeves' residence. Can I help you?" Kara hesitated, and in a sullen voice said, "I need to speak with Mr. Reeves, it's important." The lady acknowledged and in another few minutes Kara heard a man's voice say, "I'm Mr. Reeves' father-in-law. Mr. Reeves can't come to the phone." " I must speak with Mr. Reeves, it's extremely important!" Exclaimed Kara. "Do you have a message for Mr. Reeves? Because, his wife, my daughter has just been murdered and he is unable to take any calls." The father-in-law stated. Kara thought a minute and said, "Tell him that Bruce Stanton would like to meet with him at the Library this evening at 5 o'clock and will meet him out front. He couldn't call himself, so he asked me to call. Thank you." The man replied that he would give him the message and hung up.

That evening at 5:00 sharp, Matt Reeves stood on the steps of the library and gazed around as if looking for someone and began to unlock the door to the Library. Kara, sitting on a park bench across the street in a shawl, blue jeans, and a sweater, rushed to the Library steps and darted in the open door right behind Matt. Matt turned in astonishment and asked, "What's going on here?" Kara tore off the shawl and revealed herself to Matt, who had a look of awe on his face. "I'm sorry for the deception, but it was the only way I could talk to you." Kara stated. Matt looked at her with sad eyes and a frown and said, "I have been wanting to talk to you too, and I'm sorry for getting you involved in this. "Kara began by stating, " I need to know anything and everything you can tell me about your wife, her friends, her enemies, relatives, anything else which might give me a clue. You see, the police think you and I were involved in killing your wife and I have to prove them wrong. "

Matt gave a shrug and started to tell the story of when he first met Beth at college, and how he had to compete with several other guys for her attention. He tells of how attractive Beth was, but how she used her good looks and womanly ways to manipulate and use men, "It was approximately six months after meeting her, that Beth became pregnant and eventually left college and had told Matt the baby was his, and so they were married." Matt said. He had graduated soon after the baby was born, and they made plans to move to Rossville, where her parents were from and where she could be comfortable, "Beth was a loving mother and kept a neat home, but she still had eyes for other men, "explained Matt. "I caught her several times in bars, restaurants, and other public places looking at other men and sometimes getting into conversations with them. She also found ways, with her business, to be out of town a lot, or so it seemed." He went on to say, "Even after she had her second child, Beth was reputed to having an affair with some man in town, or at least of being desirable of the attentions of these men." Matt admitted that Beth had a dark and mysterious side and kept things from her loved ones. "When she began

27

her small antique business, she had advertised and visited other towns in the area, and she had gotten to know a lot of people through the business," stated Matt. "And she even dealt with people from Switzerland, who I've never met, while trying to increase her business, but still yet, she didn't make a lot of money, and I believe this is part of why she still needed me." He continued. Matt continued telling of Beth's love for her family and he told of how she had friends, but none were very close. "I can give you a list, if you like, and you can see for yourself." He stated. Kara then says, "Well, someone got close enough to her to kill her and, I don't know if it was love, jealousy, or hate, but I do know I'll need to look at everything." Kara asked, "What was the fight about at Bruce Stanton's party the other night?"

"The same old thing as usual. I caught her flirting with a another man and I became jealous, but this was fairly normal." Matt replied.

"You know that makes us look even more like suspects, don't you?" She added.

Matt became defensive and said, "She claimed she was just brushing some lint off this other guy's pants and there was nothing to it. What would you have thought and done in my place? Do you want me to help you with your investigation?" asked Matt. She replied, "No, I think that would only implicate us further. Besides, Bruce has offered to help, if I need him. I do have one more question before we leave. Was there anyone, that you know of, who would want to kill or harm Beth?" Matt made a face and a tear came to his eye as he said, "No one could have hated her enough to kill her, maybe teach her a lesson, but not kill her."

Kara left the Library, being careful not to be seen by anyone, since it obviously would look bad if she and Bruce were seen together with all the suspicion which was now around them. As she made her way toward her apartment, she noticed a police car parked around the corner, near her apartment. Again, Kara covered her head and shoulders with the shawl and started toward the apartment building and once entering, gave a look back to see if she had been seen. After being certain she had not been seen, Kara went upstairs and entered her apartment, where she immediately grabbed a notepad and pen, and began making notes on what she had learned so far, especially, what she had just learned from Matt. She thought to herself, "Certain things did not add up." As she spoke out loud. She continued to think that for instance a small antique business would not usually be dealing in an international market, and if Beth fooled around with other men as much as Matt said, with no guilt or fear of being found out, either he was a fool, or they had some sort of agreement. Also, as much as Beth was supposed to have played the field, undoubtedly, she might have come into contact with someone causing enough hatred or jealousy to make him or her want to kill her. Exhausted from the day's events, Kara decided to get some sleep and tomorrow she would go to where they found Beth's body, since Kara didn't want to leave any stone unturned due to a lot was riding on solving this and clearing her name.

The next morning, Kara took her shower and had a bowl of cereal and proceeded to get dressed. She was anxious to get started, but she wandered how she would get in the crime scene area, since the police had cordoned it off to the public. Then, it came to her, she would pose as a reporter. After dressing, she grabbed her purse and made sure her library ID card was In there and began to open the door, but to her surprise, there stood the chief of police with a sort of smirk on his face. "Going somewhere?" he asked sarcastically. "You know you're not to leave town," he added.

"Did you need something, chief?" Kara asked.

"I just wanted to ask you a few more questions and remind you that you're still my best suspect." He declared. "The night of the party, did you meet with Matt Reeves afterward at any time?" he inquired and went on to say "I know you met him at the library last night. What is it with you two, doing things out in the open to bring more suspicion on yourselves? Are you covering up for someone else or what?"

With this, Kara replied, "We're not covering up for anyone and I had to discuss something with Matt last evening, because as you know full well, we work at the same place. And I came home with Bruce, my date, the night of the party, and after he left, I went straight to bed. Now, if there's nothing else, I have somewhere to go." With that, the chief grunted a little under his breath and walked away. Kara watched him drive away from her window, turned to get her things, and left hurriedly. The body was found at the park, about two blocks from Matt's home and was within walking distance from Kara's apartment. As she proceeded to the park, she could only guess at what she might be looking for at the scene of the crime. She needed to find something, anything, that would help to prove her innocence, since obviously, the police already believed she had something to do with it and had stopped looking for clues to who might have really killed Beth.

Upon arriving at where Beth's body had been found, Kara saw only one policeman. As she approached, she could see that he wasn't aware of her. She spoke to him in a soft voice, " officer, you look tired, have you been here long?" He replied, "Since four this morning and I still have three hours to go." Kara decided to talk awhile, so as to put him at ease. "This is where the body of that woman was found isn't it?" she asked and went on, "I thought the police had already been over this area."

"We still need to continue our search for any clues that might have been missed in the outer areas, but I doubt if there are any." He declared. Kara continued, "What exactly did she die from? Do you know, or is that privileged information? After all, I don't want to cause you any trouble." The officer then stated reluctantly, "The cause of death is still undetermined until all the autopsy results are in, but there is some speculation that she may have been poisoned due to there was no blood at the scene, but nobody knows how it happened." Kara felt the time was right and said with an authoritative voice, "Well I'm a reporter, and I need to look around, if that's no problem." With this, she flashed her I.D. card from the Library, very quickly, and stuffed it back in her purse. "Well, I don't know, I guess there's no harm as long as you stay outside the ribbon," proclaimed the officer.

As she walked around the perimeter of the crime scene, Kara was searching for something, anything that looked suspicious, or that might be a clue to the mystery which she had been dragged into. As she moved about the bushes and trees, she noticed gum wrappers, cigarette butts, and such, but although these might be clues, they could have been from anyone at any time. Continuing on, Kara moved deeper into the park to a point about thirty feet from where the body was found. And, while working her way through the bushes, she caught a glimpse of some-thing shining through some leaves and undergrowth, and as she reached out to grasp the object, she could tell it was a coin of sorts, but it was unlike any coin she had ever seen before.

CHAPTER 3
More Than Meets the Eye

This coin was of a dull metallic alloy with inscriptions on both sides in Arabic, Latin, or some foreign language. The coin also had an image on both sides. One side had an image of a mallet or hammer, she couldn't tell which. The other side had an image of columns, such as the ones built in front of museums, government buildings, etc. The object was a little larger than a U.S. quarter and smaller than a U.S. half dollar, and it had the color of a penny. Kara thought with more observation, that this was definitely unique and was probably a clue. Kara pocketed the coin and continued searching for more clues. As she moved back to the path, she noticed a small clearing with a bench about ten feet from where she found the coin. She approached the clearing, looking and watching for more clues, but found nothing. Entering the small clearing, she surveyed the area and saw a wooden bench nestled beneath some trees and footprints all about the ground, indicating this was a popular meeting place and she wandered if any clues found here would be significant or meaningful. She viewed the scene and saw that there were two or three items that could be clues, or at least were worth investigating. These were the remains of a Hershey candy bar, which could be a possible means of poison ingestion, a faded Rose with stem attached, also a means of poisoning, and a tube of lipstick that someone had lost or forgotten, still another means of poisoning. After a few more minutes of searching, Kara decides this is the extent of it and prepares to leave, but then turns toward where the officer is stationed and asked, "Was there any sign of a struggle around the crime scene, where the lady was killed?" He spoke without hesitation saying, "No, but the body could have been moved." With this, Kara turned and began walking away toward her apartment, noticing another officer in a car, staring at her as she left the park.

Back home, Kara threw her purse, coat, and shawl on the bed and moved to the refrigerator to get an apple and began to snack. While eating the apple, she couldn't help but think that something was still missing in this mystery and quickly brushed the thought aside, realizing that the mystery was still young. There were questions not yet answered, such as what was Beth doing in the park that evening and who would she have been meeting? She flashed back to the clues she had found earlier at the park. These clues indicated only that whoever met Beth could have been either male or female, and there was not yet a way of determining which it was. She did believe that there was only one person that met with Beth due to the lack of any more evidence to the contrary and also, she believed more than one or two people gathering in the small park would have raised suspicion, and if a person was attempting to kill someone, the last thing they would want, is to create a lot of attention. As she contemplated all this, she opened her purse to reveal the clues she had found and believed to be relevant as possible evidence in the murder of Beth. Kara's thoughts came quickly, and she would have to have each of these items checked out more thoroughly to see if, indeed, they were clues or just bits of trash left in the park. First, she would have to find someone who was an authority on coins, such as the one she found, and decided what better place to look than a coin collector's shop. As for the other clues, she had found, they would need to be tested to see if any poison was evident with any of them. Kara decided that she would have to travel to Chaffee for a nearby coin shop and then to St. Louis for analysis of the other clues, since a bigger city would have the most updated equipment for such a procedure. She needed to call Bruce, since he said he would help if he could and now, she will need him for a field trip to further the investigation. Immediately, she picked up the phone and called Bruce at his office. Bruce answered as a Real Estate Broker would answer, "Stanton Real Estate, how may I help you?" Kara replied, "Bruce, this is Kara and I need to ask a favor, but I want to ask in person. Could we meet for dinner this evening about 7:30 at Maurice's to discuss something?"

"Well, I have an appointment at 7:00, but I suppose I could call them and move the appointment. What's up?" he said.

"I'd rather discuss it later, if you don't mind. See you at dinner, bye, bye," stated Kara, and she hung up to get dressed.

Later, at Maurice's, Kara entered and caught sight of Bruce's blonde hair and edged her way toward him. Bruce stood up when Kara arrived at the table and gazed at her with curiosity. He signaled for the waiter so as to order a couple of drinks. "What will you have?" He asked her. After ordering drinks, Bruce, by this time very anxiously queried. "I haven't seen you in a while and then you call with a proposition for a favor, what can be so important?" Kara replied. "I don't know where to start, but here goes. I've been doing some looking around at Circle Park, where Beth's body was found, and I may have come up with something. I need you to take me to Chaffee and St. Louis to confirm something about some clues I found." Then she removed the coin from her purse, gave it to Bruce and said, "This was near the place the body was found, hidden in the brush. It's so unique, that it has to have a bearing on the case. But only someone who deals in coins could tell me what I need to know." Bruce examined the coin, turned to Kara and said, "I thought we had an understanding that you wouldn't go snooping around by yourself. You could be hurt or worse." Kara grabbed the coin and replied, "If you don't want to help me, I'm sure Matt will. Besides, you haven't seen how the chief keeps insinuating that I killed her or at least had something to do with it. He believes I had something to do with Beth's death and he is determined to get me for it. Did you know, he even has officers tailing me everywhere I go?" Bruce sort of moaned and complied, stating, "OK, I'll help you, so you don't get into any trouble. What time do you want to leave in the morning?" She replied without hesitation, "Seven." With that Bruce smiles, and they began discussing the menu with the rest of the evening being fine food and small talk.

The next day, as the two entered Chaffee, Bruce and Kara stopped at a small cafe' for some coffee and browsed through the phone book. There were two listings for coin shops, so Kara wrote the information down on a slip of paper and after finishing their coffee, they left to find the first coin shop, named MO's Coins and Collectibles was closest according to a map they had acquired at the café, so they tried this one first. When they arrived at the shop, they saw a small, older man with wire rimmed glasses behind the counter and glanced at the display cases aligned around the store. "Can I be of some service?" he asked. Kara reached inside her purse and produced the odd coin and asked if he was familiar with this type coin. The shopkeeper took the coin, put it beneath his eyeglass, studied it for a few minutes and apologized as he spoke saying, "I'm sorry, but this coin is foreign to me, and I couldn't tell you much about it." Then he continued saying, "You might try my competitor in town, they deal in specialties and imported type coins and artifacts. They are located on the other side of Chaffee in a rather questionable area of town. You'll see when you get there." With that, he gave some directions, and Kara and Bruce thanked him and left the small shop. Soon, the twosome were near the other oddity and collectibles shop known as The Emporium, and as they became closer, they could understand what the previous shopkeeper meant by questionable. This part of the town was older and not well kept. Some buildings were vacant and boarded, but there were still some businesses and shops open and ready for business. The Emporium was a small shop with a warehouse behind it and was open to the public, so Kara and Bruce opened the door to the shop and slowly walked in. At first sight, the two saw collectible items on one side of the store and about four coin cases in front of the counter with more unique items on the other side. There was no one behind the counter as they could see, but at the moment they began to look around, out came someone from behind a curtain in back of the counter. It was a man, of what looked to be of Indian descent, dark hair and eyes, and a tattoo on the side of his neck of a coiled black snake. He nodded at the couple and simply asked "Help you find something?" Kara approached the man with the coin in hand and said sheepishly, "We would like some help with determining what kind of coin this is and its worth, please." She handed the coin to the man with outstretched hand and waited for a response. The man took the coin and examined it and said in a stern voice, "Where did you come across this coin?" "I got it from a friend" replied Kara. "Why, what is the meaning of the coin?" The storekeeper responded, "Well, this coin originated in Scandinavia where it was first associated with a legend of a Norse Mythical God Of Thunder who, it seems, used to fly a chariot with winged horses across the skies creating a thunderous noise in preparation for a Rain God, which was associated with fertility. The Inscriptions on one side is for home and peace and the other side reads, strength and war." He continued with, "The worth on these coins vary as to who will pay the most and can range from $100,000 to $150,000 to the right party. I could make you an offer of $75,000 and collect the coin immediately, if you so desired." With this, Kara insisted, "I believe we'll hold on to it for a while. But, thanks anyhow." And the two turned to leave the shop when the storekeeper said, "I suppose an increase in my bid would tempt you to sell the coin?" Kara shook her head as if to say no, and then continued to walk out the door as Bruce followed close behind. Inside the Bruce's car, Kara began talking, saying "It's no coincidence that this coin was lying in the park where Beth's body was found. There has to be a connection and we need to find out what it is ASAP." Bruce agreed as he started the car and began to drive away. He then said, "Where to now?" Kara looked over at Bruce and stated, "We can't do anymore right now, but we can check on the analysis of the clues, I found, tomorrow at St. Louis. For now let's get a couple of rooms and spend the night, since it is getting to be pretty late." After making a pit stop for some beverages, Bruce and Kara located a motel to their liking and decided to check in for the night. The motel was not an expensive one, but looked nice both outside and inside and offered the rooms they needed. The time now was 9:00 pm and it was too early to sleep, so after checking in, they decided to talk about what had transpired earlier in the day and have a few drinks. Upon arriving at Bruce's room, he suggested this, "Why not come to my room and we'll discuss what we learned about the coin and try to piece together what the coin and Beth had in common?"

"Alright, I need to freshen up a little, and then I'll meet you back here at room 211,"

Kara replied and then walked down the hall to her room 213. Kara returned to Bruce's room within ten or fifteen minutes and knocked on the door of 211. Bruce came to the door and motioned for Kara to enter upon opening. She sauntered in and turning to Bruce asked, "Do we really have any more to talk about, excepting what we already know about the coin?" "Yes, and by the way, are we certain the collector was truthful with us?" Bruce replied. "But, it does not matter if we have anything to discuss or not. I figure we have to eat, and so I ordered some food for us, which should be arriving very soon." He went on. Before Kara could get another word out, they heard a knock at the door and Bruce went immediately to open the door. There stood a waiter with a cart and a tray of food. Bruce tipped the waiter and proceeded to the cart to lift the lid on what was prepared and revealed two filet mignon steaks and salads and a bottle of wine to drink with the meal. Bruce looked at Kara, who was smiling at the sight she was seeing, and said, "Dig in." And he proceeded to pour some wine into Kara's glass. She sat down in front of one of the plates and started to eat some salad and then moved to the steak. There was not much talk, since both were very hungry and the meal hit the spot. But, all Bruce could do, while eating, was stare at Kara longingly, and wander if she may feel the same toward him.

CHAPTER 4

Getting Down To Business

After dinner, the two laid back in their chairs to express their fullness and satisfaction with the meal they had just eaten. Kara thought that this was perfect so far and began wandering if the night was going to bring anything else. Just then, Bruce stood up and exclaimed, "This is not what it looks like." "I just thought we should eat and discuss some of the important facts about the case and the clues you found." Kara grinned and stated, "Well, it does look as if you went to a lot of trouble to get me alone with you." And she sort of chuckled and said "How did you know I was thinking along those very lines?" He responded by saying, "I didn't want you to get the wrong idea. Here I am in a motel room at night with a beautiful woman and well, you know what I mean?" Kara stood and moved toward Bruce, saying, "I could say the same thing. Here I am in a motel room, late at night with a handsome man, and I can't deny my attraction to you. So, what should we do about this situation?" Bruce, without a word, moved toward Kara and kissed her slowly and lightly on the lips. Kara leaned toward Bruce as he took her in his arms and began kissing her more intensely as he ran his hands over the curves of her hips and moved slowly up and down her body with touching and embracing. He then found the buttons of her blouse and began loosening them one by one until he was able to pull the blouse off her shoulders and let it drop to the floor. She responded by unbuttoning Bruce's shirt and pulling hard to get it off and threw the shirt to the floor beside her blouse. Kara next went to Bruce's belt and began to unfasten it, almost as if she were in a hurry. Meanwhile, Bruce is moving his fingers in a way to unfasten Kara's bra, and once this was done, he let it drop to the floor and moved to her slacks and began to unfasten and let them drop to the floor, also. Kara kicked her slacks aside, and she began tugging on Bruce's pants to remove them in a similar fashion. Now, the two were wrapped up in each other, cuddling, intense kissing, and feeling each other's bodies in a way as to express their desires for one another. It was then that Kara took the initiative and maneuvered Bruce toward the bed as they both laid on the bed entangled with what would be their first night of sleeping with each other. And, before the thought of the case at hand or any reservations Kara may have had about being with another man could present itself, she found herself enjoying the pleasures of having sex with Bruce, which made everything all right for the time being. The lovemaking went on for hours as the two fell back in exhaustion when finished and quickly fell into a peaceful sleep.

The next morning, Bruce had arisen earlier than Kara and had gone to the lobby, where he found breakfast was being served in the restaurant area. He picked up some pastry and fruit and some coffee to bring back to the room where Kara was still sleeping. When he finally got back to the room, Kara was up and had showered and was nearly dressed. "Want some coffee and doughnuts?" asked Bruce. Kara nodded yes and took a cup of coffee from Bruce, saying " We need to get going soon. I'm anxious to see what the results will be on my findings." Bruce agreed and the two continued drinking coffee and snacking on some pastry. Finally, Bruce said, "About last night, I don't want you to think it was presumptuous of me, I couldn't help myself." Kara laughed and stated, "Most men are that way, but I felt the same way and without any regrets. I thought it was wonderful." They finished up and then packed up their things and met at the car, where Bruce states, "I suppose we'll head for the forensic lab when we arrive at St. Louis and see if we can get some information on where to go from there. This is where GPS comes in handy and I couldn't have asked for a more beautiful navigator." Kara smiled and commented, "I'll bet you tell all the girls that, especially the ones you've just slept with." Bruce smiled and placed his hand on Kara's knee and replied, "No comment and I don't mean anything by it, I don't know what to say." They both laughed at this and continued driving. St. Louis was about an hour away now, and the conversation had turned to the previous day and how the shopkeeper had offered a lot of money for the coin. "You know, if I didn't need this coin to solve this mystery, I'd have pretty much thought about taking the shop owner up on his offer."

Upon arriving at St. Louis, the two searched for the downtown area where the Crime Lab was supposed to be located and wound up on a street they had never heard of, naturally, and saw a sign outside a building indicating they had come to the right place. They jumped from the car and hurriedly moved toward the entry door. When inside, they saw a round man sitting at a desk and he had a security badge and shirt on making it obvious that he was in charge of entry. Kara smiled and said, "Could you please direct us to the forensic science department of the Crime Lab?" The security officer replied, "It's not that easy. First, I need to know what business you have here and who are you?"

"Kara Steele and this is Bruce Stanton, and we are here to have a precious metal and some other items checked for any kind of clue as to where they are from or an identity of previous owner. You see, we believe one or all these items may have involved in a crime and we need to find out all we can about them," she replied.

"What kind of crime are you talking about?" the guard stated. Kara glanced at Bruce and stated, "We aren't certain if they are involved, but the crime was a murder of a friend of ours." The guard rose from his chair abruptly and picked up one of the phones on his desk and dialed a number. He then spoke to someone and then after a short silence, he hung up the phone and said, "You'll have to wait a while. Please have a seat and someone will be right with you." She leaned toward Bruce and asked, "Do you think we made a mistake by coming here? Do you think we should leave?" Before he could answer, a small framed woman with dark hair and a comely appearance came up to them and uttered factually, saying, "Sorry for the wait." "I'm told you have clues to a murder and you would like them analyzed. Is this correct?"

"Yes, but you probably will need a little more information regarding the situation." Replied Kara. She went on saying, "You see, we both come from a smaller town and are both connected to the victim, who was killed. And, we both have been approached by the police in this small town as being suspected of having something to do with her death."

"This could be due to the fact that we are both fairly new in town, and we both knew the victim. Anyhow, we have been doing a little digging and we came up with some possible clues. We won't know anything until they are processed. Do you know how long it will take to evaluate these items?" Kara dug through her purse and produced the coin, the partial candy bar with wrapper, the rose stem, and the tube of lipstick, and she proceeded to explain that Beth was poisoned and she thought possibly one or more of these items could be a clue. The woman replied, "My name is Margaret, and I can do an analysis on these items, but I warn you, I'll have to inform the proper authorities of these possible clues, and that they may truly be pertinent to a murder case. Your names and any association with the case will be revealed through processing of the files, and so you may be required to turn these over to the police investigating the murder." Kara looked at Bruce and says, "Well, we would have to go to the police at some time anyhow, wouldn't we?" Bruce nodded in agreement and turns toward the woman and states. "Go ahead and process, and we will deliver these to the police ourselves, if they are indeed deemed to be clues to her murder.

"The woman then says, "It will take about a full day to analyze these items. Will you be staying here in

St. Louis, or will you go back home and have us ship the items and results to you?" Kara replied, "I have another day or so, before I need to get back to work, and I'm sure when I tell Matt why I haven't been in to work in a couple of days, he'll understand." She turned to Bruce and asked, "How about you, do you need to get back or should we stay and retrieve our items tomorrow?" Bruce immediately replies, "I can handle my business from my phone and laptop for another day. I say we stay and return tomorrow." Bruce gave Margaret his cell phone number and politely, the two said their thanks and gave orders to call as soon as there was any news. With this Kara and Bruce left the building and proceeded to get into Bruce's car, when Kara noticed something odd. There was a black sedan parked across the street from them and she happened to notice the passenger looked a lot like the man from the shop where she had gotten the estimate from regarding the coin. "Bruce, does that look like the shop owner we talked with yesterday at Chaffee?" She blurted out. "I believe he is trailing us." Bruce looked over at the car just when the passenger side window, which was tinted, was closing. He said, "I don't know. I didn't get a good look." "Let's go and see if he follows." She states. As Bruce and Kara pull out, the black sedan begins to follow. A few blocks away, Kara suggests to Bruce, "Let's turn onto a main highway and maybe we can lose them." Sure enough, as the two pulled onto a major highway, the black sedan was stopped by approaching traffic and could not follow. At that time, Bruce puts his car in high and they begin to pull away from the sedan, quickly. "If we get back into the city right now, they can't find us, and what's the meaning of why they're following us, anyhow?" Bruce exclaimed. Kara replied, "It has to be something to do with the coin. I have a feeling that the coin is more valuable than what we were told, and those guys aren't just riding around town on their day off, they want the coin."

CHAPTER 5

Another Clue

While riding down a side street of the city, Kara and Bruce began planning their next strategy. Bruce, finally breaks the silence with "It's beginning to get late. I think we should fill up my car and find a place to stay the night, or do you want to go back to the same place as last night?" "No, I believe the shopkeeper followed us there last night. I say we find a different place, more secluded, maybe at some exit off the main highway." She replied. So, the two got back on the interstate and began looking for an exit where they could get gas, something to eat, and also a place to spend the night. They didn't have to drive far before they came across the Arnold exit, which offered all they needed. Upon exiting, they pulled into a service station and Bruce filled the car with gas, while Kara went inside to ask for the best motel to stay at in the near vicinity. The attendant was very helpful and told them the best motel was a block away and offered live entertainment after 9:00 pm and a bar & grill for those who wanted to eat. This sounded like the right place, being off the main drag and offering food and a room for the night.

The couple got back in their car and drove the block to a small motel called The Country Home and proceeded to park in an inconspicuous parking place and headed for the front desk. Once there, Kara spoke and said, "We would like to have a room at the rear of the building, near an exit, if you have something?" The clerk gazed at her chart and said, "I believe I have something on the first floor room 146 and how will you pay this today?" Bruce spoke up "Cash, and can you point us to the restaurant?" The clerk took the money and pointed down the hall, saying, "The Wanderer, as it's called, is just down the hall and your room is the other way." As she pointed toward the rooms in the motel.

Bruce and Kara peered at each other and started toward the bar and grill, due to they hadn't eaten since early in the morning. Once they are seated, the waitress of the place asked, "Can I get you something to drink?" Kara responded with, "I'll have a light red wine and a water with lemon with my meal." "And I'll have an Ultra Lite beer and also, a water with lemon. Thanks." Bruce added. "This is a quaint little place, don't you think?" asked Kara. Bruce didn't say any thing at first, and then he began by saying, "Those men that were following us were pretty, sketchy, and if they followed us to the other motel last night, they will probably go back to get our names and will be able to trace us back to Rossville. I have a feeling we aren't out of the woods yet." Kara replied, "We will have to take it as it comes while looking over our shoulders at every turn, unless we go on the offensive and place an anonymous call to the police about a possible smuggling ring located at that particular shop. That might buy us some time tomorrow. Especially, since they followed us to the Crime Lab and will probably be staking it out to see if and when we would come back." Just then, the waitress came back with their drinks and asked for their orders. The two ordered and sat back to enjoy their drinks. It was after 4:00 when they leaned back after eating and talking. Finally, Kara stated, "I am going to the room to rest a while and maybe take a nap. Do you want to join me, or do you have something else to do?" "As a matter of fact, I do have to check in with my answering service and make a few calls for later this week. I'll join you in a little while, ok?" He reached over and gave Kara one of the two keys and said "See you later."

As Kara moved down the hall toward the room they had rented, Bruce ordered another beer and pulled his phone from his pocket. He then dialed a number he was familiar with and let it ring a few times before someone at the other end answered, "Hello" said the person at the other end of the phone. It was a familiar male's voice. Bruce hesitated, and then said "Hello."

Bruce continued, "How have you been Matt? I thought I would check with you to see if there were any new developments with the case and to see how you're holding up." There was a pause and then the voice of Matt, sort of sullen and depressed, "The only thing new is that the police are asking where you and Kara have disappeared to, and since I'm a suspect, they have been grilling me especially hard. They believe we are all planning some sort of escape or something." He went on, "When will you be back? And, have you found out anything, yet?" At that moment, Bruce paused as his waitress approached with another beer. He thanked her, and as she left, he spoke into the phone, saying, "We do believe we are onto something, but I can't go into it over the phone. We will have to wait another day to get the results from the Crime Lab, and then we should be coming back to Rossville." With that, the two men said their good-byes and got off the phone. Bruce finished his beer, left a tip, and headed for the motel room.

Upon arriving at the motel room, he looked around to see if anyone was watching or following and entered the room. There he found Kara, already in her nightgown, lying on the bed. She was awake and as Bruce entered, she spoke, saying, "I couldn't get to sleep, so I decided to wait up." She continued with, "Did you have any messages or appointments?" Bruce shook his head as to say no. She went on, "You look troubled. Do you want a nightcap, or do you just want to get some sleep?" Bruce said no to the drink and started for the bathroom, saying, "I need to freshen up a little and get some sleep." At hearing this, Kara threw back the sheets on the other side of the bed and began to turn off the light as Bruce maneuvered his way toward the bed. When in bed, Bruce lay on his back thinking of the day's turn of events. Kara could see he was distressed, and began to help him unwind by first telling him, softly, that he shouldn't worry about it right now, and she began to rub his chest with her fingers while kissing him gently on the lips. Then her lips and tongue slid, slowly, down his chest to his belly button, where she lingered for a moment, until Bruce bent down and kissed her on the mouth, a firm and long kiss. He then did the same to her as she had done and within a minute or two, the couple were entangled together in embrace and sex.

The two completely forgot why they were even at this motel. They were lost in love and sex and this continued for about forty minutes with them both heaving upward and gasping at the moment of climax.

The couple awoke the next morning and as Kara pulled back the curtains, they could see bright sunshine coming through the windows. It was about 8:15 am, and so, they both began to get ready by taking showers and brushing their teeth. And, while putting on some clothes, Kara said, "The Crime Lab should be opening by 9 a.m., since the Lab doesn't take a day off, and we should be there when it opens, so we can get back to Rossville before we're missed." Bruce, attentive to this, stated, "We are already missed by the police in Rossville. I spoke with Matt last night and he said they were asking for us." Kara replied, "Why didn't you tell me?" He said, "I didn't want you to worry and there's nothing we can do about it, not yet, anyhow." Kara was thinking how thoughtful it was for Bruce to hold back on telling her this, but she also knew that they were in this together, even more so now, after becoming lovers.

After checking out of their room and leaving the motel, Bruce and Kara drove back to the downtown area and to the Crime Lab, which was already open. They rushed in, looking over their shoulders, and looked back as they entered, but didn't see anyone. They looked at each other and figured their ruse had been effective. The police must have visited the small Emporium at Chaffee and scared the people who were following them and had caused them to abandon their following of Bruce and Kara.

Upon entering, the two came up to the same desk as before, but there was an older man, thin and tall, waiting at the desk and he asked, "Can I help you?" Kara spoke up, saying, "We were here yesterday, and we left some items for analysis." And, they began to describe the items. "Yes, replied the man at the desk, but a couple looking a lot like you two had come in at 8:30 am, when we first opened today, and claimed the items." Kara and Bruce looked at each other, as if surprised, and said, "But, how could that happen?" The man went on to say, "They gave us the proper names on the register and described the items well enough to let us return them to their owners." "But, we are the owners!" exclaimed Bruce. Kara thought for a moment and asked, "Can we at least get the results of the analysis?" The man thought for a second and said, "That's the least we can do." And, he started rummaging through a file folder of the past week's work. Then, he spoke up, "Here we are." "This is what you need, I believe. Let me make a copy." Kara looked at Bruce and whispered, "We know where the coin and other items are, and we need those results." After the transfer of the analysis of the coin and other items to Kara, she grabbed Bruce's hand and they rushed out, saying, "I only hope we aren't too late to get the evidence back from the Emporium."

The next thing Kara and Bruce had to do was come up with a plan to get back what was stolen from them by the shady artifacts dealer. So, they decided to drive back to Chaffee and find a quiet place to come up with some idea as to how they were going to do it and when, since time was of the utmost. The ride was quiet for the most part, each of the couple knew what had to be done, but weren't sure as to how. Their conversation went like this, "We could go directly to the dealer and threaten him with legal action." Stated Bruce. "Or, we could simply go to the police and get them to go with us to the shop." Suggested Kara. The two continued to drive and talk. "Wasn't Beth's vocation an antiquity and collectibles dealer?" Kara presumes. "Yes, and Matt may still have access to her business cards and any promotional material, she may have had when she was killed," concluded Bruce. They were on the same page as to what might be a way to get to the valuable coin, which is also a clue in the murder of Beth. Their thoughts became voiced as Kara declares, "If we can get Matt to use some of Beth's business cards and whatever else that would be handy, we could create a plan to get the coin back." So, they had a half- baked idea to get the coin back, since this is the only thing that seemed to matter to the Crime Lab, because of its monetary worth and origin. The couple had learned the other so-called clues were of no significance. In other words, the coin is considered to be a motive for Beth's murder, and it is necessary to have this piece of evidence to remove suspicion from Kara, Bruce, and Matt, also.

CHAPTER 6
The Retrieval

They had a plan, not a very good plan, but at least, it was something. "So, the plan is to use Matt as the contact with the crooks to offer a huge amount of money for the coin. But, how do we get Matt in with them enough so they'll bring out the coin?" Asked Bruce. "Leave that to me." Replied Kara. As the two came closer to Rossville, they became more apprehensive about the idea. "We would need Matt to be with them and without reservation, for he would be putting up a front for the thieves, and he needs to be very convincing." States Kara. "The idea is to make them believe the coin came from Beth's company to begin with, and then find a way to retrieve it. I have some ideas that might work." She says.

Later, as the two arrived at Rossville city limits, they noticed a crowd was forming at the Library's front entrance. They quickly stopped the car and ran over to the crowd and asked, "What's all this about?" to one of the people standing out front. "Matt Reeves has put out an announcement that there are more clues, and that the case of his wife's mysterious death will be solved soon." Said the onlooker. Kara said, "Bruce, can you believe this? What's

Matt thinking? We need to talk with him. Now." The couple began edging their way toward the front of the Library until they were at the door. Seeing the two, Matt swung the door open to let them in, saying, "Can you believe this? All I did was tell the Chief, that I believe we have another clue to Beth's murder, so he could stay off our backs. He's been hounding me to no end to find out where you two were and to make certain I didn't leave town." Kara looked at Bruce and said, "Well, the damage is done, but, we don't exactly have the clue, due to it was stolen from the crime lab. I will tell you all about it, later." At this time, the elderly Ms. Abbott, the librarian, approached and asked, "Do you need to leave, Mr. Reeves? I can take care of this. I'll tell the crowd that you have already gone and that you would rather not talk of the matter just yet. That should curb their curiosity for a while. And, I, personally, want to express my regrets about your wife, and if you need someone to talk to, you can count on me for moral support." Matt responded with, "You have always been there for me, Elaine. Thank you very much." Elaine was Ms. Abbott's first name. It seems, she had never married and was considered the town's most notable spinster.

"Let's meet at Mitchell's Restaurant in about 15 minutes and go over some things, if that's ok with you two." Kara voiced. And with that, the three headed for the back door, so as to not be stopped by the people outside.

Upon arriving at Mitchell's, Kara, Bruce, and Matt moved toward a table in the corner near an exit and had a seat in the booth. Kara started the conversation with, "We found a collectible coin in the park and had it analyzed and valued. It is rare and worth a lot of money." "How much money are we talking about?" Asked Matt. "Over $100,000, we believe. But, there is a catch. The coin was stolen from the crime lab and we have to get it back." Replies Kara. "You see, to get the value, we had to visit the Emporium dealing in rare collectables, and to make a long story short, the people there are less than honest and managed to follow us and steal the coin." Bruce retorted. He went on to say, "We need your help to get it back." "Whatever it takes, I'll do it. Anything to prove we had no involvement in Beth's demise." Stated Matt. Then, Kara and Bruce went on to explain that the coin, found in the park where Beth's body was found, could have been a motive for her murder. And, that almost anyone could have done it and at this point, Kara gave a notable revelation, saying, "You know even the Emporium dealer, or someone like him, could have killed Beth over the coin. She did deal in collectables, did she not? And if we can prove that someone else had a reason for killing Beth, we may be off the hook." Now, all that was left was to hone their plan so as to get the bugs out, and therefore not make any mistakes. If these people were capable of killing, they probably wouldn't hesitate to kill again. Kara spoke again saying, "You are the key to getting the coin back, Matt. We have to make them believe you or Beth had some item which was more valuable which could be traded for the coin." Matt replied, "There just may be something in Beth's shop which we could use for that. Let's run by there when we finish eating and have a quick look. But, I know the Chief is looking for you. Maybe, I'll go alone not to raise any suspicion." The trio then ordered sandwiches and drinks for lunch and continued discussing how they might fool the keeper at the Emporium. Their story had to be flawless, or it could be dangerous for all of them. They knew the people at the Emporium were dishonest, and they had to believe they were also greedy. So, to fool them into giving up the coin was the only way of getting the coin back. Kara's plan was key, but it needed tweaking, and it needed to have a provision for the possibility of something going wrong with Plan A, they needed a Plan B.

After lunch, Matt left for Beth's collectible shop, leaving Bruce and Kara to go over all the points of Plan A and then to come up with a secondary plan. Kara started with, "If we can find an object which is potentially worth more than the coin, and Matt can convince them of this, along with our help of course, we can submit the coin to the law as evidence, before the shopkeeper of the Emporium is aware of the ruse. If not, we'll have to go to Plan B." Matt looked at Kara with eyes aglow and asked, "What is Plan B, and how are we going to do this anyhow?" Kara hesitated and said, "Let's go back to my apartment, and I'll try to explain what I have in mind." With that the two paid their bill and started out of the restaurant and headed for Bruce's car.

Upon reaching Kara's apartment building, Bruce noticed an unmarked police car immediately down the street and said, "Uh Oh, looks as if someone's waiting for us. What should we tell them?" "Let me do all the talking, OK?" Kara replied. While walking up to the building door, a man's voice could be heard behind them, saying, "Coming or going?" The two turned and immediately responded, "Hello Chief. Were you looking for us?" Kara went on saying, "We just came by to pick up something. What can we do for you?" The Chief looked at Kara and said,

"You two are hard to find. Have you been out of town?" Kara replied, "Well, we have been running errands. And, I have been helping Bruce show some properties. Why, did you need to see us?" The Chief again looked at her saying, "I've heard you may have some evidence related to the Beth Reeves' murder. You know it's against the law to withhold evidence in an investigation, don't you? If you do know anything, I would suggest you tell me now, or I'll find out on my own. The Crime Lab in St. Louis contacted me and said something about a couple had evidence regarding a murder investigation in our area, and the Reeve's investigation is the only one I know of." Bruce decided to interject at that time, saying, "We do not have any evidence regarding the murder, but if we do get any, we will be certain to give it to the law." "And, another thing, we have the right to some privacy, but it seems every time we turn around, you or one of your men is lurking around a corner, watching us." The Chief smiled and started away saying, "You do have that right, but we have the right to pursue this investigation in any way we like." He sauntered away and got into his car and drove off.

Kara and Bruce reached the apartment door and entered with Kara speaking first, "You know, I believe I just came up with our Plan B." Bruce, now inquisitive, asked, "Oh yea, what did you come up with?" Kara responded with, "I don't have it all worked out yet, but I think I have the gist of it, and I believe we can start working on Plan A, now."

The two sat on the couch and began brain storming ideas for the best way to handle the swap of the coin for this other item, Matt said he could get. Bruce said he and

Kara should start it off, "We need to go in first and set the table, so to speak, for Matt. We could tell them that we know they took the coin from the Crime Lab and we will call the law if they don't return it to us." Kara thought a moment and said, "No, we don't want them to get upset or angry in any way. They would be tipped off that we were trying to retrieve the coin. No, we need to go in and ask if anyone has since brought in a similar type collectable, because we know there are other items floating around." "I see, sort of build up their greed and inquisitiveness. Well, what if we tell them about some other items, just throw them out there and see what they say?" Bruce states. Kara soon after replies, "No, I'm afraid that would be too much from us. That needs to come from Matt." "Well, then we need to give Matt a good cover story and a good reason why he happened to be in this particular shop." Bruce responds. "We will, but we need more information about Beth's business and her business dealings. Matt needs to let us know all about her business including the names of her clients and/or customer list. We'll have to get everything right the first time. There won't be a second time to try to fool them, for they'll be wise to us then. Let's get with Matt and go over what he needs to do when we lay the groundwork for our little ruse." Kara responded with, "I hope he has found something we can use to entice the shopkeeper for our plan to work."

Kara pulled her cell phone out of her purse and began to punch numbers in order to call Matt. As the phone rang several times, a voice at the end of the call answered. It was Matt, "Hello" and then Kara continued with, "Did you find what we need?" "Yes, I found the pendant, called the Jewel of Athena. It's a collector's piece, which originated in Greece, and then somehow, over time, has made its way to our shop. I heard Beth speak of it numerous times before she was killed. The value is estimated at $200,000 to certain collectors in Greece." Kara says, "We need to meet somewhere private, to go over our plan and coordinate our little scam. Is there a safe place we can meet?" Matt thought a minute and states, "Yes, I believe Beth's shop is the safest place and besides, if the police are watching, they won't be as suspicious. I'll wait till you get here." Kara went to the window to look out and said, "The police are still watching, but they may not, Oh wait, their car is just now pulling away. They must have had a call to go somewhere. Let's go, hurry."

The two picked up the plans, and Kara retrieved her purse and they headed out the door.

Upon arriving at Beth's Shop, The Trade-Winds, they parked in back and saw Bruce standing in the doorway, waving them in. As they enter the shop, Matt says, "Are the police following you?" "No, but they may come looking later, let's get on with it." Bruce utters. Kara, Bruce, and Matt sat down at a table, where Matt opened a box to reveal a necklace with a pendant and a large, magnificent diamond surrounded by inscriptions, when translated, offered praises to Athena, the Greek goddess of wisdom, skills, and warfare. Kara and Bruce agreed that this would tempt the shopkeeper to trade for the coin, which they needed as a clue to clear their names after they initiated the plan. The three immediately, sat down at a table and started going over the plan, Kara had come up with to get the coin back. So, after going over the plan three times, they all agreed that they knew what to do, and that this should work. Kara asked Matt, "Do you have the client or customer lists I was needing?" Matt went to a file cabinet and pulled out a large stack of papers and said, "Here are orders and receipts Beth had over time while doing business in the Trade-Winds." Kara reached out and took about half the documents and handed the rest to Bruce, and then he said, "What are we looking for?" Kara replied, "Anything, especially anything regarding the coin." The two began sorting and reading the papers for clues. Until, Bruce interjected, "Is this all Beth had regarding customers. I sometimes keep a separate list of good customers for Real Estate. Maybe, she has something in her desk or thereabouts." Matt jumped up and moved toward Beth's desk and searched through the drawers, and found nothing, until he came upon a drawer which was locked. He shouted, "Here is a locked drawer. I'll try to pry it open, since I don't have a key." With that, he grabbed a long letter opener and began prying on the drawer, until it finally sprung open. Matt began looking and found, sure enough, a separate lengthy customer list. He took the list to Bruce and Kara, and they began scanning down the list at the names of her clients. Suddenly, Kara exclaimed, "Look at this. The Emporium of Chaffee was one of her clients." Bruce asked, "Are there any appointment dates on the list that match Beth's demise? Maybe, she met with one of her clients on the day she was killed." Matt looked longingly at the two searching the list and said, "Do you think one of these clients had something to do with Beth's death?" "I would say, there is a good chance that it's a strong possibility. And, I see here that the Emporium was to meet with Beth on the afternoon of the day of Beth's death. This is very incriminating." Says Kara, as she adds, "Not only did they have a date to meet her, they stole the coin from us, which was found near the scene of her murder, which gives them motive. We may be dealing with the murderer with our plan to retrieve the coin." "And, now we have a choice of trying to go through with the plan, or simply turn everything over to the chief and see what happens." She added. "But, if we get the police involved at this point, the killer or killers may bolt, and we may lose an opportunity to catch him or them." Bruce says. Matt and Kara nodded a yes. Kara went on to state, "My plan B, was to turn everything over to the Chief anyhow, if we didn't get the coin back. I suggest, we go ahead with the plan, but much more carefully, since these people might be more dangerous than we first thought." "What say you?" Kara voiced. Matt and Bruce both agreed, and they began to unroll the plan to get the coin back. It was Bruce, who asked, "The cost of the pendant, if we don't get it back, is that a loss to the company?" Matt answered quickly, "Insurance. No one knows but us, about what we are to do. But, if everything goes well, we'll get it back, along with the coin."

The three decided that they should separate and leave, and tomorrow morning, they would drive separately to Chaffee to the Emporium and enact their plan. After saying their goodbyes, they all left Beth's shop and went back to their respective homes. That night, after telling Bruce good night, Kara took a quick shower and was sitting in her apartment, just thinking about their proposed plan to get the coin back. She knew they would have to do some good acting to convince the Emporium shop-keeper to release the coin. Kara had taken the pendant and placed it in a safe place. Now, she took then necklace out of the safe place (the cookie jar where no one would look), and began studying it and polishing the diamond on the pendant. She could see the clarity of the stone and knew the scam they proposed had to work for everyone's sake, or they could be charged with theft. It was near bedtime, when she returned the necklace to the "safe place" and started to bed, all the while fretting about what was going to happen the next day.

The next morning, Kara woke to the sun light shining through her window. She jumped out of bed to see that the time was 7 a.m. and she must eat some cereal and get ready, because Bruce was going to pick her up at 8:30 a.m., and the two would drive to Chaffee. Matt was to follow them over there to the Emporium in his own car.

At eight fifteen, Bruce and Matt were parked outside the apartment. Kara saw them through the window and immediately grabbed the pendant, while she started for the door. She put the pendant in her purse and opened the door. To her surprise was a tall figure of a man standing in the hall. "Going somewhere?" asked the man in a stern voice. Kara, surprised, says, "Yes, we're going out to get breakfast, Chief. Is there a problem with that?" The Chief asked gruffly, "All three of you?" Kara replied, "Well, we want to discuss how much progress is being made on the case, by the way, how far along are you on Beth's murder, Chief?" The Chief grunted and stated, "We are making progress, and you and your boyfriend are still suspects, so don't get out of pocket." With that, Kara turned to leave down the stairs to the entrance of the apartment building, where she jumped into Bruce's car, and they sped away with Matt not far behind.

As they traveled to Chaffee, Kara realizes her plan is now set in motion. She and Bruce will meet with Matt outside the Emporium, where she will give the pendant back to Matt for transfer. Then, Matt and Bruce will accompany her inside to unfold their scheme. This will only be happening in about a minute, since the group has entered Chaffee and are near the Emporium, which as she could see, was already open for business. As they pull up near the shop, they can see that there are no other customers, probably due to being so early. The time to act was now, and she, Bruce, and Matt got out of the cars and started toward the Emporium. Upon entering, they noticed the shopkeeper, they had seen earlier, was examining a piece of pottery at the rear of the store. Matt laid back from Kara and Bruce so as to be perceived as coming in afterward. The shopkeeper started toward Bruce and Kara, saying, "I remember you two from the other day. What can I do for you?" Kara offered to speak, saying "I believe you may have something of ours. You see, the Crime Lab told us someone picked up our items, and we happen to know that you followed us there the day before. And, we have come to get our things back, especially the coin." The keeper of the shop looked at them and said, "I don't know what you are talking about." Kara smiled and says, "We thought you might say something like that." She turned to look at Matt, who was standing near the door, saying, "Matt, show the gentleman your credentials." Matt came forward and handed the shopkeeper a business card for the Trade-Winds and said, "I'm the new owner of the

Trade-Winds and I believe you are familiar with the company. And, I have something which you may be interested in. You see, my wife, the former owner of the company has passed and now, I am the new owner. The items you have are worth much to us, and we are here to make a deal with you for the return of the coin and other items." Bruce and Kara stepped forward a little, declaring, "We know money is your prime motivation, and we're prepared to give you a valuable item in exchange for the coin, plus the other items and maybe some cash to sweeten the deal." Bruce went on saying, "Show him the item, Matt." At that time Matt brought out the necklace wrapped in tissue, stating, "I believe this will entice you to possibly give up the coin for this property." The shopkeeper gasped, and peered at the necklace. Matt went on, "This piece, if sold to the right collector, is worth much more than the coin. Would you not agree?" The shopkeeper gazed at the necklace, knowing what it was, and declared, "If I had the coin, you refer to, could you be trusted to make this exchange?" Kara snapped at this, "Because, we need the coin and other items to clear our names, and as you can see, we came here alone with the confidence that you would cooperate." The shopkeeper hesitated, and then slowly moved toward a piece of furniture, a sort of cabinet, and took out a drawer and began to empty it. Once empty, he turned the drawer upside down and there was the coin, taped to the bottom of the drawer. The other items were in a small bag among the contents of the drawer in an inconspicuous manner. The keeper of the shop then states, "This will be an even trade, will it not?" The three looked at each other and Kara says, "We know the necklace is much more valuable, so we will trade it for the coin, the items, and $10,000 cash, and you won't see us again." The man thought a minute and went to the register with the coin and bag in hand. He then reached under the cash drawer and pulled out a stack of one hundred dollar bills. Bruce looked at the shopkeeper saying, "Are you sure there's $10,000 here?" The man told him to count it, which he did. Bruce looked at Matt, saying "It's all here, give him the necklace." And Bruce reached over to retrieve the coin and bag and money. Matt handed over the necklace and followed Kara and Bruce out the door. Kara spoke up, "I don't trust him. Let's get out of here." They got into their respective autos and started out of town and as they hit the highway and were well on their way, Kara looked at Bruce and said, "Did you get everything?" Bruce reached into his pocket and pulled out a small recorder. He then said. "Yes, and the tiny nick I put on the necklace clasp will help to identify it later."

Back at Rossville, the three decided to meet at Mitchell's to go over everything, since no one's home was safe. The police were watching them and the people who stole their items from the Crime Lab knew who they were. At the restaurant, they looked over the items and coin once again to make certain they were authentic and they were. But, Matt noticed something and said, "That lipstick looks familiar, and I believe I know why. That was Beth's. I gave it to her on her last birthday with some cosmetics." Kara asked, "Are you sure? This could be another clue, even though it isn't the murder weapon." He replied, "I'm sure. She must have dropped it. Did you say that you found it at the murder scene?" "Yes, and if I'm right, she was either surprised, while putting on her lipstick, or she dropped it to leave us a clue. But, I'm still not certain as to how the coin, which is obviously a clue, could play a part in this mystery." The group gathered up the evidence and stashed it away, as they decided to let Matt keep the coin in his office at the Library, because he would be less conspicuous holding it. Bruce would keep the recorder with him, since he could say he used it for appointments. And, Kara kept the bag of possible clues, due to they didn't want it all kept at one place for security reasons. It was getting late, when Kara suggested they go home and get a good night's sleep. Little did they know that they now possess the keys to the murder of Beth Reeves.

At home, Kara hid the small bag of evidence in the "safe place" and went about her proposal to get a good night's sleep by first taking a shower and then going to bed. But, as she was getting out of the shower and drying off with the towel, she heard a knock at the door. She put a robe on and started toward the door, where she shouted, "Who's there?" A voice, she recognized, came through the door, "It's me." And, upon hearing the voice, she proceeded to open the door. It was Bruce, "I can't sleep. Can you sleep?" Kara replied, "I was just about to go to bed." "Oh" Bruce continued with, "I should go then."

CHAPTER 7
Another Chapter

As Bruce is standing in the door and Kara is standing in a bath robe, the two look at each other and laugh a little. She finally says, "Come on in for a while. We'll talk about the case, if you like?" Bruce answers with, "I'd rather talk about us, you and me." Kara glances at Bruce and says, "You know, I care for you, but I've had bad dealings with men in the past. And, it isn't you, it's me. I just don't trust myself to get involved again." Bruce asked, "Do you have anything to drink?" Kara rises from the couch, where she was sitting, and moves toward her kitchen, and pulls from the refrigerator a pitcher of tea, and at that moment, Bruce asked, "Anything stronger?" She opens a cabinet drawer, reached for some Brandy, saying, "You know, I didn't say that to hurt you. I really am fond of you, but you don't know anything about me." Kara began telling him of her past marriage and relationships, and she also told him she had decided to not be involved with another man. And, when he heard this, Bruce pronounced, "That's fine, not with any other man, only me." And, this could only mean that Bruce didn't care about Kara's past, and the present was all that mattered to him. Bruce went on to say, "The past is gone, and all we have is today and tomorrow. I feel very strongly about you. You know that, don't you? And, I believe you feel the same way about me. Am I right?" He sipped his drink as Kara paused a little and then said, "I do care strongly for you. It's just that I'm afraid of what may happen." Bruce set his drink down and moved toward Kara, saying, "We can't live with a fear of the unknown. We simply must live for the moment, sometimes." With this said, Bruce eased toward Kara and reached for the ties to her robe. He then pulled one of the ties loose to reveal Kara in her under clothes. Bruce moved closer and removed the bra, covering Kara's breasts, which now were showing signs of arousal with the pert breasts' nipples becoming more firm. Bruce's hands now were moving over her taught breasts and sliding down to her panties, where he began to remove her panties, ever so slowly, and Kara was responding with a relaxed movement and some sultry groans. As Bruce continued to take her panties off, Bruce too, was becoming aroused, and he kneeled and paused slightly, as he became closer to her torso/belly with his head directly in front of her. She became very excited as Bruce was breathing on her thigh, and she couldn't help but put her hands on his head as to help him maneuver to her midsection. They made love for a few moments, and then Bruce calmly rose to begin taking his clothes off. Now, Kara was in the moment and began helping Bruce remove his shirt and belt to reveal him in his underwear. He then pulled his underwear off, and she pulled the robe off and let it hit the floor. The two stood looking at each other naked, and each began touching each other as their foreplay heightened, and they laid on the bed. Bruce began moving his tongue over Kara's breasts and toward her navel, while Kara rubbed his ears softly and quickly. By now, both were very excited, and the lovemaking began. When it was done, the couple fell into a sound sleep wrapped in each other's arms. The next morning brought sunshine and moderate temperatures. And, this was a work day for both Bruce and Kara, even with the mystery still needing to be solved. Kara was up first and making coffee, while Bruce was getting dressed. He still had to get to his place to shower and change for the day. The two sat for a while and had coffee and toast, while discussing the clues, and how they were to come together like pieces of a puzzle. But, the time caught up with them and Bruce said his good-byes and kissed Kara on the lips and was out the door.

Kara began getting ready by showering and getting her clothes for the day in order. After she had finished dressing, she checked on her "safe place" to see if her stash was still intact, and it was, so she returned the jar to its place and grabbed her purse and headed toward the street. All the way to the Library, Kara's thoughts were torn between the mystery at hand and the relationship, she was forming with Bruce. But, to her, the mystery had to come first. As she neared the Library, Kara could see Matt arriving and standing at the door, as if, waiting for her. She reached the door of the Library and says, " Hello, is everything ok?" Matt replied with, "Yes, I believe everything is working out." Kara knew what Matt meant by this and replied, "Good, because I'm a little worried about what to do next. Could we sit and have a short talk?" Matt replied, "Come by my office in fifteen minutes, and we'll have a quiet discussion, if you like?" Kara nodded and proceeded to enter the Library. Upon entering, she went directly to her station, where she usually worked, and began shuffling library cards. Soon, Ms. Abbott walked by and noticed Kara was a little distressed and asked, "Is everything alright, dear? Do you need anything?" Kara replied, "No, I just need to speak with Mr. Reeves for a few minutes. I have a lot on my mind these days. You know the police consider me a suspect in the Beth Reeves homicide?" Ms. Abbott paused a moment and said, "I'm sure everything will work out, even if they don't find the culprit, they can't very well charge you if there's no evidence or witnesses to the murder implicating you. I don't know that much about it, but I do know they haven't charged anyone, and they're still looking for something, I don't know what. Maybe, there will be a revelation in the case and the suspicion will be diverted elsewhere. Who knows?" She continued, "You know, Mrs. Reeves met and knew a lot of people, and anyone of them could have been the murderer. The police must realize that." Kara replied, "I know, but as long as Matt, Bruce, and I are suspects, the police look less at others and are trying to concentrate on us, and that is a big weight on our shoulders." At that time, Kara remembered that she is to meet Matt in his office. She, politely, excused herself and headed directly to meet with Matt.

When at Matt's office, she entered and closed the door behind her, saying. "Matt, I needed to tell you a few things that are on my mind, and the best time is now. I believe some of Beth's clients may have had something to do with her death, either directly or indirectly. I'll tell you why. The amount of money the business was generating on those collectibles was great, and just like the Emporium stole from us, I believe Beth could have been a target, due to one of her artifacts, possibly for the money, or for another reason." Matt listened intently, and said, "I can understand that, and I believe the police should have come up with that a long time ago. But, they looked at her books and found nothing to suggest any of the clients on her lists would stoop so low as to kill, when they could buy or steal an item, as the case might be. When the Chief spoke with me, he insisted it was a calculated murder, and he said jealousy or passion was obviously a prime motivation in this case. But, we know that's not true, but how do we get him to look at others for suspects?" "I know what you mean, and I've been thinking about it. I need to get with you and Bruce again to go over my thoughts, but I believe I have an answer to our problem." asserts Kara. "But, another thing," Kara continued, "is that I'm going to need to take time off until this thing is settled. It could be a day, a week, or longer, but I can't work under these circumstances. So, I'm asking that you lay me off for an indefinite time, so I can wade through this to get some answers." Matt looked over at Kara and said, "You may have a point, since we are both suspects for now, maybe we shouldn't be together as much, for the sake of less suspicion aroused." Matt and Kara agreed to meet discreetly to go over any new information or evidence. Kara did want to have one more meeting with Matt and Bruce at present. She started for the door, saying, "We should all three meet at the park, where Beth was killed, so I can go over something with you. Shall we say about six o'clock this evening, just after dark. After all, the police have taken down their do not disturb signs and are not really watching the Park now, anyhow." She then contacted Bruce and the meeting was on.

That evening, at dark, the three suspects met at the Park, not really knowing what was to be found out by this, but Kara wanted to see something that hadn't been brought out yet. Kara was first to speak, "I'll tell you why we're here. Beth was killed by poison, and it is my belief, one of the clues I found at here was used to carry it out. The only other way was if the killer took the murder weapon with him or her or them." Bruce asked, "What are we looking for, anyhow? We could have gone over this somewhere else, couldn't we?" Kara states, "I have a scenario and want to play it out to see what you two might think." She led the two over to the bench near where Beth's body was found and says. "Suppose Beth and the killer, or killers, had a date to meet here that night for whatever reason, and Beth had been putting on her lipstick, when the killer or killers came up on her and grabbed her, causing the lipstick to fall into the brush. And, then he, she, or they held her while forcing her to ingest the poison. And, the motive for this could have been a number of things such as, the murder could have been a robbery gone bad, or maybe, because of something she knew, she was a threat, and someone felt she needed to be eliminated, or, and I say this due to her reputation as liking the men, that she had a date here with a man and there was an argument, maybe a breakup, and he happened to come prepared with a poison to end her life." "There could be other scenarios, but these came to mind, and I believe that very soon, we should let the Chief in on the clues and our suspicions, so he will be looking for the true killer or killers." Kara finished. Bruce spoke up, saying. "I agree, and I hadn't thought of it that way, the three ways the murder may have happened. But, I also think we should let the Chief in on all that has taken place and the clues, we found earlier." Then, without warning, a voice came from several feet away, "Well, what do we have here?" It was the Chief. "I have all my suspects at the scene of the crime. They say the killer or killers will always come back to the scene of the crime, and here we are." Matt said angrily, "Wait a minute! We came out here to help you do your job right." Then Kara chimed in and began repeating to the Chief everything she had just told Bruce and Matt. Bruce states, "We have some clues we found here, that your people missed along with these ideas of who else may have been the killer, and all you can think of, is us." The Chief paused a while and said, "Bring me those clues tomorrow morning, while I give this some thought. And, don't leave town." He says as he turns around to leave.

The next morning found Kara, Bruce, and Matt gathering their respective clues from their hiding places, which had kept them safe from discovery. And they all met at the Police Station, where the Chief was waiting for them. And he said, "Well, maybe you can explain the nature of these clues. You know what they are, where you found them, and how they are connected to this case, in your opinion." The two men looked at each other and they turned their gaze to Kara, who started with, "The clues all came from the Circle Park. I found them after your men searched the area where Beth was killed. A couple of items were just trash, such as the candy bar wrapper and the rose stem, as we had them tested at the crime lab. But the coin and the lipstick, which I found in the bushes, have a connection with Beth. The coin is an expensive, collectible piece from Beth's shop. And the tube of lipstick was a gift from Matt to his wife sometime before the murder. We thought the poison was administered through one of the clues found at the Park, but none of the items tested positive for poison. We knew some of the items had to be connected, and with some detective work, we found the connections. There were some circumstances surrounding the coin and lipstick, as these clues were stolen from the lab. We learned who stole them and made plans for their retrieval, and here they are. But, we need to fill you in on the rest of our story. Since the killer or killers are still out there, we know now, that one or more of Beth's killers could be from her client lists, and we have that also. Bruce and Matt can fill you in on the rest of the information in order for you to look elsewhere for the murderer. By the way, do you know how the poison was administered to Beth?" The Chief replied, "By mouth, but it was otherwise undetectable with no odor or nothing found in her system which could identify it. The only way we know it was an oral administration is, because there were no needle marks and she was in perfect health according to the Coroner." Kara nodded, as she headed for the door and left the office. She had some other matters to check into. Besides, she could check with Bruce and Matt a little later. She had decided to pay a visit to the local drugstore and maybe the hardware store, to try to pinpoint the sale of any questionable poison drugs of late, knowing it was probably to be found somewhere else, other than a store of any kind in the near vicinity. Her search led her to the local pharmacist, whom she had seen at Matt and Beth's party, but had never met. As she entered the small store, she came up to the counter and immediately introduced herself. "Hello, I'm Kara Steele, and I am here today to ask a few questions regarding drugs, which could be determined as poisonous, taken orally, and easy to acquire. A friend of mine was recently poisoned and we need to track down as to how it happened, and I was wandering if you could help." The owner and pharmacist replied, "Didn't I see you at the Stanton party a while ago?" Kara went on, "Yes, I recently moved to Rossville, and took a job with Matt Reeves at the Library." She continued, "After Beth's untimely death, we have been trying to determine who could have done this and how. Matt, Bruce Stanton, and I have been trying to decipher the mystery of her death. And, which brings me here to see if, possibly, you knew of any kind of drug, which could be used in her demise." The pharmacist, a middle-aged man with a touch of gray in his hair, a distinguished look, and an educated vocabulary, stated, "My name is Blake, Blake Summers, and I am very pleased to meet you, but I wish it were under different circumstances." "And, yes there are several types of drugs which could possibly be used as to what you have described" And, as Kara intently listened, the pharmacist began writing a list of drugs, which could be used as a poison and which were medically acceptable for treating certain ailments with a Doctor's care. "But, these drugs can only be acquired by a prescription and only in small doses." Blake went on to say. He then handed Kara a list of three names of certain drugs, and he again stated, "These are several, which might be used. There are more, but, acquisition, costs, and being less common, I didn't see where these others would be as notable per your request." With this, Kara gave her thanks and stated, "It has been a pleasure to meet you and I hope we meet again." And, she turned and left the shop with the list. Her next stop was at the local hardware store, where she, upon entering, noticed the store had several customers ahead of her, so she decided to look around some on her own. She strolled past the herbicides and poisonous controllers of pests, such as, rats, rodents, and other vermin. All of a sudden, a female voice from behind Kara, asked, "Can I help you?" Kara turned to see a young woman in her mid to upper twenties, who she recognized from the small Deli Restaurant, she had visited when she first arrived at Rossville. The female went on to say, "Oh, I remember you from the restaurant, when you first arrived in town, and the local welcoming committee, namely, Linda Kaplan and her friends greeted you. Your name is Kara isn't it? What can I do for you?" Kara returned her question with, "Yes, Kara Steele, and I remember you also, but, I didn't get your name." The woman replied, "My name is Kim, Kim Creel. My dad owns this store, and I help out occasionally." Kara quickly says, "It is very nice to meet you." "I'm looking for a poison, which could be used as to kill someone. I know you have heard about my boss's wife, Beth Reeves' murder. Well, the police suspect poison as the method for the killing. I am just gathering information as to what may have been a possible agent used to kill her. I need to know if there is something, sold over the counter, which could be administered in a low dose, that could be taken orally and could kill within a short time, maybe within a few minutes." Kim thought for a minute, and said, "I can think of only one good prospect, and there may be others, but the one I'm thinking of is so common. And, that would be arsenic, but it takes longer than minutes, it would be at least a couple of hours after ingestion to kill. There could also be a different type poison of as to how you described, which is not sold over the counter, but could be obtained illegally on certain websites." Kara replied with, "Thank you so much, and it was nice to meet you. I hope we will be seeing more of each other." As she started toward the door and turned to wave a farewell, she says, "Good-bye."

The next thing for Kara's research is to get on the computer as to find a website on the internet that would have other possibilities for the acquisition of a fast-acting poison, which could be suitable for Beth's murder. But first, Kara decided to do some other needed research at the Library, where she worked. Once there, Kara entered the Library to find Ms. Abbott working diligently at her desks. Kara asked, "Have you missed me? I'm sorry not to have been more help at work, but you see, I needed to take some time to try to clear my name, as well as Matt's and Bruce's." Ms. Abbott inserted, "Is there anything new? I mean with the case, or should I ask? I'm being a little nosey, I know." Kara replied, "No not at all. The police say it is suspected that Beth was poisoned somehow, and we, meaning, Matt, Bruce, and I have been working to clear our names, as you may already know." Ms. Abbott, again, "Yes, I knew you were trying to discover more evidence in the case. Did you find anything else out?" No, not really.

We have some ideas about some questionable dealers of antiques and collectibles, Beth had dealings with, but we don't have anything really concrete at this time." Ms. Abbott says regrettably, "That's too bad. I wish you luck." Kara again replies, "Thanks, I just had a couple of things to look up in the library, and I'll be leaving again. Is there anything I need to do before I leave?" "No dear, it's been slow and I'm pretty well caught up. Can I help you find anything?" replies Ms. Abbott. Kara shook her head as to say no and began heading toward the long line of shelves, storing the books of the Library. She then came to the book she needed located in the middle of a tall bookshelf. She looked around for the portable steps, used by the employees to insert and extract books from the shelves. She found what she needed and climbed upward to pull out the book entitled, "Herbs, Plants, and Other Such Earthly Information". She then put the book into her purse and began walking to the exit. Suddenly, Ms. Abbott appeared and asked, "Did you find what you needed?" Kara replied, "Yes, I believe this is all I'll need, thanks." And with that, continued to walk toward the exit and out of the building.

As Kara walked down the small town's streets to her apartment, she felt as if someone was watching and following her. But, she shrugged off the feeling, and to herself, explained it as a case of nerves. Once arriving at her apartment, she entered and went straight for the couch and began reading in the book, she had just gotten from the Library. Kara was looking for special details, which could be used to tie into the murder investigation, but she didn't want to declare any suspicions or information, until after she had done some more research. She read through some of the chapters of the book pertaining to herbs and plants, which could be used for poison. She found what she needed and began to search on her laptop the same methods chemicals, both herbicides and medicines, could be used as a poison.

Meanwhile, Matt and Bruce had been getting interrogated on the case, as to what they were doing and why they thought they could go beyond the law to investigate Beth's murder. It was going in this manner. The chief states, "Just who came up with the ideas for finding possible new evidence at the park, and then instead of reporting it to me, decided to take it upon themselves to test this so called new evidence at St. Louis and then confront the thieves who stole this evidence? And, who is to blame for planning to get the evidence back without even checking with me or my people, before you initiated the plan? You put yourselves in a great amount of danger. What if these people who stole the evidence were the murderers? What would you have done if they had decided to kill you for being involved? And, exactly, where did Ms. Steele run off to, just when I wanted to get some answers?"

Bruce and Matt peered at each other for a minute or two, and then Bruce spoke up and said, "We all had a hand in it. We all decided something had to be done, since you and your people assumed each of us was a suspect, and you were paying more attention to us than the case and not looking for other suspects." The chief responds with, "I have only been following police procedure, and as a matter of fact until I have all the evidence, everybody, including you three, are suspects. And, I will be looking into all aspects of the information and clues, that you all have been so kind as to turn over to me." With that, Bruce and Matt stood to leave, and Matt states, "My wife and I had some rough times, but I loved my wife, and I would never have done anything to harm her." The Chief stared at both Matt and Bruce, and he declared, "Just remember, you are all still being considered in my investigation, so you have been forewarned. Have a good day. I'll be in touch." The two men walked out of the chief's office, and headed downstairs toward the street. Upon reaching the door, Bruce says to Matt, "I think he still believes one, or all of us could be involved in your wife's murder. There's no convincing someone with that type of mentality. We will probably have to continue to solve this mystery, if we ever want to have our names cleared." "I wander how Kara is doing?" asked Matt and continued with, "Maybe we should call her and sit down for another talk."

In the meantime, Kara is searching for the method and poison used in Beth's demise. She finally comes across a poison befitting the crime, while searching the internet. Ricin poison, is made from herbs and plant life at home, and is virtually untraceable, both odorless and tasteless, when done right. The key elements can be found almost anywhere. All someone would need to do is find an agent, or poison, which would cause an immediate reaction, thus killing almost immediately after taken into the body, a sort of catalyst. After some researching, Kara learned that certain viral encoded enzymes could be used as a catalyst, and which could have been used to trigger the Ricin and caused a shorter time period of reaction after ingestion. If this was the method of poisoning, it would have had to be someone with some intelligence and other scientific skills to make it work quickly enough to kill almost instanta-neously. At that exact moment, Kara's phone rings, and as she picks the phone up she realizes that it's Bruce on the other end and in a relaxed voice, says, "Hello, Bruce, did you need something?" He replies with "Yes, Matt and I have just left the Police Station, and we were wandering if we could get together for another meeting and discuss our options at this point." Kara says, "Sure, where would you like to meet?" "Somewhere that doesn't cause a lot of suspicion." Bruce replies. "Let's meet at the Pizza House downtown. There won't be many people at this time of the day." "Ok, we'll meet you in about fifteen minutes." Bruce responds.

At the Pizza House, the three sit at a table at the back of the building where there are no people and very lit-tle foot traffic, and Matt begins by saying, "We were in-formed by the police chief, that we are all still under suspi-cion, and are still along with everybody else, suspects. Do we have any more ideas on what our next move should be?" Kara starts, "Well, I have been doing a little research the past few hours, and I think I have a sort of profile of what our murderer might be. At least, I think I have a few characteristics associated with the killer. He or she is prob-ably someone Beth knew or had met before. The killer, or killers, might be educated and knowledgeable of chem-istry and biology, and certainly, very intelligent to come up with this method of murder. Or, this could have been a planned murder for hire type killing by someone who didn't want to get their hands dirty. There were still a lot of unanswered questions." Bruce calmly asked, "Do you have any idea of where the killer, or killers, were from?

That could possibly help to clear up some of those questions, we still have to answer." "No, except that, since Beth probably knew her killer for him or her to get close enough to her to administer the death potion, I'd say he or she was from here or at least in a close proximity to Rossville." Matt then asked, "What about the poison? Do we know anything about the type or the way the poison was given to Beth? I can't believe this is all happening. It seems as if the world is unraveling around us. Should we be looking more at the dealers and customers Beth had?" Kara replied with, "Certainly, those people are on our list of possible suspects, and now the Chief is on to them as well. We'll have to wait."

CHAPTER 8

Follow the Clues

Their meeting didn't result in any great solutions as to the mystery at hand, but it did give the three sleuths a more definite insight on what needed to happen for this crime to be solved. First, now that The Chief was in on the clues, they must make certain that they didn't get in the way of the police investigation, while they conducted their own little query. After all, the Chief, who suspected all three of them for the murder, had not even turned over any other clues that could be helpful in clearing them, or he hadn't told them of any other clues which might be out there. This only meant, the police didn't seem very capable in the past, and Kara, Bruce, and Matt would need to continue to resolve the murder, and who could have done it.

They all decided to return to work the next day, Bruce would return to his Real Estate Office, and Matt and Kara met at the Library's door steps the next morning in time to open the doors. "Does it look like we're making any progress, or are we still kind of in a stall?" asked Matt. "No, we have made a lot of progress, but there are a lot of questions, and we don't have many suspects. Actually, the only ones we know of that might have had interests in the coin, or in Beth's business, are the people who stole the coin from the Crime Lab, and who we had to pursue to get it back." Stated Kara. She went on to say, "But, since we gave these findings to the Chief, he should be looking into their alibis and any other information he can gather on them." Matt nodded and they both started toward their offices. As the day continued, nothing but the case at hand could be of any importance to either of them. Matt worked on his duties of making certain the Library was operating profitably, and Kara fumbled through her work in an effort to get something done. She and Ms. Abbott did some inventory and some logistics, there-by locating some older books and setting up an arrangement to sell the unwanted books to a buyer, which the Library had sold to before. This kept their minds on something besides being totally on the case.

At day's end, Matt, Ms. Abbott, and Kara said their good-byes, locked the Library's door. Then each walked away toward their own destinations. Kara arrived at her apartment, which was not too far from the Library, and went inside. Upon entering, she kicked her shoes off and began to look for something to eat. Looking into the refrigerator, she noticed some cheese in a package and decided she would have a grilled cheese sandwich and a bowl of soup. She went to the cabinet, where she kept the soup, and started rummaging around, moving cans around to finally find a can of tomato soup. After eating, she went to the couch and relaxed a bit, before reaching for her laptop. She got online with her computer and typed in the Emporium of Chaffee to see what she could find. What came up didn't surprise her. There was the website for the Emporium and several reviews flashing, and each one declared warnings of dealing with this particular business. It seems the people operating the business were already under suspicion for some shady dealings in the area. Kara thought this is what she would find, and she could even imagine them being involved with Beth's death. About this time, her phone rang, and when she picked up, she could see it was Bruce. She answered, "Hello" and immediately, "Have you heard? Those people, we had to retrieve the clues from, were arrested and accused of Beth's murder." He said in one breath. Kara replied, "No, I haven't heard, but I found some warnings about them on the internet. Did you hear anything else, maybe what proof there was against them, or anything?"

"No, nothing has been released yet." He said.

"But, I suppose we could go to the Chief and ask if he has any proof."

"I'll meet you at the station in about fifteen minutes," says Kara. After getting off the phone, Kara was not convinced that these were the killers, since the method did not seem to fit their style. They are more, crude and would not have taken the time to do what was needed to do this killing. She realized that though the method wasn't their style, they could have hired someone who used that kind of technique, since whoever did it was very meticulous and deliberate about it.

As she closed the door behind her, Kara rushed down the stairs and exited the building onto the street. She looked up and saw Bruce in his car. He shouted, "Get in", and flung open the door for her. She slid into the sports car, and they were on their way to the station. "I decided to pick you up, since I was already in the area," Bruce spoke. "What proof do you think the Police could have against these people?" He asked. "Nothing that we know of, except maybe the residue of the poison or the apparatus used to concoct the poison," she replied, "Anyway, I'm getting tired. Could we go somewhere to rest some?" With this, Bruce made a right turn and began toward his home, which was nearby. As the car cruised down the residential street, Bruce glanced over at Kara, who was resting her eyes, and he thought to himself how beautiful she looked at this moment. Minutes later, the car pulled into the driveway at Bruce's house, and he stopped the car in front of the detached garage. He then reached over to touch Kara, gently, on the shoulder as to awaken her. She immediately looked at him, and they both got out and started toward the front door to the house. As they reached the door, Bruce opened the door with his key, took Kara's hand and led her into a near-by bedroom, where he laid her on the bed and covered her with a blanket. She fell off to sleep in an instant, and Bruce turned to go into the other room.

Bruce pulled out his cell phone and called a number. A woman answered saying, "Police Department, can I help you?" Bruce said in a low tone, "Could I speak with the Chief, please?" The phone rang a time or two, and a male voice spoke, "What can I do for you?" It was the Chief. Bruce introduced himself, saying, "This is Bruce Stanton, and I have a question for you. Is there any reason why Ms. Steele is still under suspicion? She has worked very hard to clear her name and involvement in this case, and I don't see any reason, with the current developments, why she should be put under any more scrutiny. It's obvious, she had nothing to do with the murder, and all she has done is try to help clear it up." There was a pause. Then the Chief replied, "What you are saying does seem to be true, but, I still have a homicide to be solved, and I don't have any conclusive evidence that suggests that I release any of you as suspects. Therefore, I believe I will just continue to keep an eye on your little group, at least till I have something to go on to make an arrest. That is, if you and your friends don't mind." He added. "Now, if there's nothing else, I'll be getting back to work. "And he hung up the phone.

Later that evening, as Kara was waking from her sleep, Bruce was in the kitchen preparing a Goulash. She entered and asked, "What smells so good?" And she moved directly toward the range top to have a look. Bruce moved slightly to give her room to look, and stated, "It is something I picked up from a master, my aunt." Kara responded, "It looks very good, as does the chef, if you know what I mean." Bruce turned to look at her and saw a smile come upon her face. "It looks as if you feel good after your knap, do you not?" he stated. She continued smiling and nodded a yes signal. He continued, "We could put the Goulash on simmer, if you want?" She wrapped her arms around him and said, "Well, let me think a little on it. Ok, I've thought about it. I'll race you." And she started toward the bedroom, with Bruce not far behind. She was removing her underwear, when she said, "We really should stop meeting like this." And, then laughed a little to send a message of sarcasm. When fully unclothed, the couple stood in front of one another and began moving their hands up and down the curves of their nude bodies. This went on for a few minutes, and then progressed to their genitals. Their arousal was evident with both, and while still feeling and moving their hands over each other, the two inched toward the bed and laid on the bed gently together. More foreplay followed, until Bruce became more aggressive as the two began to devour each other's bodies and finally moved into a position of intercourse.

When their lovemaking was completed, they both lay back on the bed, exhausted to be sure. They rested a while on their pillows, until Kara said, "You know, I wasn't really expecting this to happen. But, I believe, that I may be falling for you. I think about you and us much, more than I ever thought I would. My time spent with you is more fulfilling each time we're together." Bruce replied with a kiss on her lips and saying, "I believe we were meant to be." They talked a while, and Bruce includes that "We need to eat, the Goulash is getting cold, and I need to check on some contracts, potential buyers, and you know, work." They ambled back into the kitchen, after dressing, and Bruce started the burner for the Goulash to warm it. In a few minutes, the food was ready, and they were famished and began eating. Afterward, Kara was picking up the dishes to wash and also putting the food that was left in the refrigerator. "You know, you don't really know a lot about me. After all, we only met a short while ago, and I just recently moved here. Are you certain, you would be thinking of me in the same way if my past was more evident to you?" Kara asked. "I admit, I have been holding back on purpose. You see I've been married before and divorced. And, the fact is, the divorce was my fault. I was a promiscuous wife, and my husband was beaten up due to my indiscretions. But, I do have to say in my own defense, that I've changed from that spoiled, insufferable person, I had become. Since I've been here and after meeting you and the people here, I've become more satisfied and content. Of course, you are the main reason for this change. I'm only hoping you can look over the way I used to be." She added. Bruce hesitated and responded, "You know, you didn't have to explain anything. We are both adults, and I'm no angel, I have to say. And, yes I can overlook your past, if you can overlook some of the stuff, I've done. You know, I'm falling in love with you, and I'm hoping you feel the same way." They kissed each other a long kiss and continued to clean the kitchen.

Later, Kara was looking over some of her notes regarding Beth's demise and noticed that something didn't seem right about how the poison was administered to Beth. Why would the killer or killers go to all this trouble to poison her, instead of just killing her with a different type method, such as a gun or knife? There must have been a reason why this type of murder was done instead of by other means. Did it mean that the murderer or murderers knew her very well, and the selected means to kill had something to do with this. Kara started going over the crime scene and the clues again in her mind. Why was Beth killed in the Park? Was this a clue also, or was it just convenient for meeting with her? And, the coin and other clues, were these really significant, or were they a part of some coincidental happening, that took place at the same time as the murder? These were all questions, which hadn't been addressed yet, either by her or the police. Could it be they had all been thinking the wrong way about the case until just now?

The next day, Kara woke to find, she had fallen asleep on the couch, still mulling over the clues and the questions, she had considered. But, none of the questions seemed to have any answers that made any sense. She decided to shower and dress for work. Until now, Matt had been really lenient with her work status, and the reason why was evident, but she now needed to get back to making some money. The time off had hurt her pocketbook and bills would soon be coming in.

She arrived at the Library right on time. Matt and Ms. Abbott were opening the doors to the building, and turned to say good morning. "Could I see you in my office, Kara?" Matt asked. Kara nodded and said, "I'll be up as soon as I put my things away." This was her purse and notes regarding the case. After dropping off her things at her desk, Kara went quickly to Matt's office, where he was waiting. The first thing he asked, "Have we done anything else on the problem of who killed my wife?" Kara began explaining, "I have gone over all the clues, and I have come up with more questions than answers." She continued, "Maybe, you could shed some light on one or two of these questions? Now, I know the Chief has asked this, but is there anyone who may have hated Beth enough to want to kill her?" Matt began to answer, when Kara stopped him and said," Hold on, what I mean to say is, is there anyone that was close to Beth, who may have wanted to kill her? And, that could be for money, love, or anything at all." Matt shrugged and said, "I have given it a lot of thought, and I only have the same answer. It could have been a past lover, business partner, a client, a customer, anyone she knew or knew her, or knew of her. She wasn't well liked by some, but I never had an inkling of anyone who would want her dead." Kara then says, "I believe the Chief and investigator are on the wrong track, and I think I will do some more investigating on my own, that is, if I can get some more time off. But, I have costs and bills coming in soon, and I will need some kind of advancement on my salary, here at the Library, if this is possible?" Matt replies, "I can't justify any monies going through the Library, but I can give you what you need from my own account, and don't say you can't take it, because, I feel somewhat responsible for you being in this situation." "And, you have done everything you can to help find the murderer." He continued. Kara drops her head and with a somber tone in her voice, responds, "I don't like the idea, but I'm sort of desperate. My bank account has decreased, since I moved here, and I really need and like this work opportunity, you've given me. I don't know why this had to happen, but I do intend to find out." Matt nodded and says, "I'll tell Ms. Abbott, you will need some time off for personal reasons, and I'll ask if she can do some of your immediate duties." With this, Kara started out the door and turned to say, "Thank you." She then went to her desk and began making a list of items she was and would be working on for Ms. Abbott. At this point, she realized an urgency in trying to solve this mystery, and she put the list on Ms. Abbott's desk and began getting her stuff together. Ms. Abbott had noticed the list and asked Kara, "Dear, what is this list doing on my desk? Are you wanting my help?"

"Yes, Mr. Reeves and I have discussed this, but he will be telling you all about it, and I wish to thank you in advance for all you've done." "I'm hoping and praying all goes well, and I'll be back soon." Ms. Abbott responded, "May I call you or drop by your place, if I need any assistance?"

"Of course." Says Kara, and immediately, she writes down her cell number and home address and gives to Ms. Abbott. Now, Kara picks up her belongings and starts out the door, waving good-bye.

As Kara is walking down the street to her apartment, she realized that she needs to call on Bruce. She starts dialing his phone number and then a thought comes to her. She is walking and could amble by the Circle Park, where Beth was killed, since it is in close proximity of the Library and her apartment.

Arriving at the Park, Kara went to the place of the crime, knowing any evidence would now have been compromised, but she felt, that she might get a different viewpoint of what may have happened. She immediately noticed how the Circle Park, notably called this due the physical nature of the Park, being surrounded by a circled road, which is around the perimeter of the Park of about three acres in size, is close in proximity to about anywhere you may want to go, by foot or vehicle, in Rossville. This made Kara believe the Park was a place of mutual convenience for whoever met with Beth at the place of her demise. And, now, why were they meeting? Was it business, love, or, something else? Now also, to figure out who it was, she met with, that fateful day. A lot of unanswered questions, she thought and time to resolve.

CHAPTER 9

What's Really Going On

As Kara looked at the site of the murder, she reconstructed what she had found before, and where the items, she had found, were situated. The bench had not moved and the brush and lawn had not changed. And, the three paths, leading to the bench, had not changed, but she thought, why hadn't she investigated the paths, seen where they lead, and whether anything could be found out? Then she remembered, the police had suggested she leave, before she was finished looking around. Kara gazed at the three paths and thought the most logical path for her in this case is where she had found the coin. So, she started down this path, and she noticed something peculiar. There was a small enclosure with a cov-

er to protect visitors to the park from rain and such. She decided to look inside and found a few items left by past persons. These proved to be just little things such as gum wrappers, cigarette butts, and a couple of pamphlets about the town of Rossville, none of which seemed important or pertinent to the case. Still, these could be additional clues to the discovery of the killer or killers. Kara found an empty envelope in her purse from a previous bill, and she began collecting the remnants of a person's or persons' trash, as this is what it all was. Kara collected all the items she found, and began surveying the surrounding area to see if she missed anything. Suddenly, she glanced toward the rear of the small enclosure, and something caught her eye. She moved toward the object with a deliberate pace and stride, until she reached the area where she spied it. Then, she bent over to pick up a sparkling piece of a type plastic. Kara observed what she had found and noted that it was a woman's small cosmetic case with nothing in it, and it was slightly worn from the rain and sun, and on the outside was printed in small letters, Abby. Kara, flashed back to the tube of lipstick, she had found on a previous search. Now, these could be coincidental, and yet, both were found close to where the body was discovered. And, now, there was a name which could be significant, if these were associated with the case. Next, she must tell Bruce of her discovery, and see if he might be thinking the same as she is. Kara continued to look for anything else that might be related to the investigation, but couldn't find anything new, so she decided to head home. On her way home, Kara called Bruce saying, " You busy? I've found something else at the Park, but I don't know if it is viable or not. Why don't we have a brunch, and I will show you this last piece of possible evidence? And, then we can decide on whether to go talk with the Chief." Bruce hearing this, replies,

"I'll meet you at the Diner in say, 15 minutes, OK?" Kara responds, "OK."

At the Diner, Kara and Bruce sat at a booth at the rear of the small eating place, so they could discuss the situation without prying eyes or ears. After ordering, Kara reached into her purse to retrieve the small cosmetic case and immediately passed it to Bruce, saying, "This was found near the site of the murder, but in a small roof covered shelter near the bench, where Beth met her end. Do you know of any women in town or that Beth may have been associated with, named Abby or possibly Abigail?" Bruce stared at the item for a short while, and said, "I don't know of any just now, but I believe we should look into it. And, maybe, we should let the Police in on it, since they do have more access to records and people than just me, you, and Matt." Kara exclaimed, "I forgot to tell Matt of my findings. I know he wants to be kept up to date on everything. After we've eaten, we should call him and tell him. Maybe, we'll simply ask him if he knows of anyone by the name of Abby. And, I'm not so certain as to telling the Police, due to they will want to take the cosmetic case as they took all the other things we found." Bruce agreed, "True, and where are those clues now, sitting, and the case is also just sitting."

After eating and paying for the brunch, Bruce and Kara sauntered outside into the sunshine, and Kara began dialing her phone, calling Matt. Upon answering, Matt asked, "What's up, anything new?" Kara replied by telling Matt everything she had told Bruce until she got to the part about the name, and she asked Matt. "Do you know of anyone named Abby or Abigale, That Beth may have known through personal or business association?" "No one comes to mind. but, I wasn't privy to all her communications and associations with people, clients or people she met with," admits Matt. Kara ends her call with, "Keep thinking about it, and let Bruce or me know as soon as you have come up with anything." As Kara ended the call, she turned to Bruce to say "Let's go to your place and go over everything again. We still have pictures of the clues, even though, we don't have them in hand." "That's a good idea," says Bruce, "I have some business to attend to also."

Upon arriving at Bruce's house, the two were having a cup of coffee, when Kara spoke up to say, "There's so many possibilities of who the murderer might be. Let's go over some of the most likely and see if we can weed some of our possibilities down to a lesser number." After hours of going over the clues, the different scenarios, and any other evidence which they were privy to, the outcome was still not clear to them. Maybe there just wasn't enough evidence to point to any certain possibilities, except what they had known or what they had believed when they started sorting through the clues and hypothesis pertaining to the case in the beginning. The facts were at hand, first there was a murder. Second, there were a number of clues, whether or not substantiated. Third, there were (according to the police) a number of suspects, everybody is a suspect. And fourth, prime suspects were anyone who knew the Reeves, Matt and Beth, which also left a broad list to decipher.

Later, the two had become tired from all the examining of the case, as they saw it, and decided to lie down on the bed for a short nap. But, as they lay on the bed, Kara leans over to kiss Bruce and with this he says, "What's that for?" Kara replies, "I just wanted to thank you for believing in me and helping me through all this." He pulls her toward him and gives her a kiss, and this was not a thank you kiss, but a passionate kiss, demonstrating a desire and lust for her, which she automatically responded to with a loving caress. Now, these two lovers became very heated and were touching and fondling each other, and this continued for several minutes. They were wrapped up in the moment and kissing hard. Kara then without words began to unbutton Bruce's shirt, and once she had undone the last button, she began on the trouser button. All this time Bruce was hurriedly undoing Kara's blouse and pants. In a short time the two were making love and deeply involved with one another. When the lovemaking was over, they both laid back on the bed and fell asleep in quiet exhaustion.

All this while, Matt was scouring Beth's books for the name, Abby or Abigale, or anything else which might lead to more information on Beth's death. Matt had searched through all Beth's business documents before, but a second look couldn't hurt. He had decided to go back to the clues, which the group had already found and research. As he got to the background data on the coin, they had found, there in plain sight was the word, abbey, the place the coin was last located. The name of the abbey was obscured by a spilled stain on the paper, where the name would have been. "Could this mean something?" Matt spoke out loud. He then digitally dialed his phone for Kara's number. "Hello Matt, did you find something?" asked Kara. Matt began telling her of the connection the coin had with an abbey. Kara thought for a minute, and says, "We need to know more about the abbey, a name, or location. You may have to keep digging through her stuff to see if anything else comes up." Matt agrees and ends the call, so he can continue to look. His search proved no other mention of the abbey was noted. Meanwhile, Kara and Bruce discussed the connection between the coin and the word abbey, even though the spelling of abbey and Abby, on the case, was different, these might have been changed in an effort to conceal the coin, sort of a code, used for the carrying the coin by the holder in a hidden manner. It was a long shot and may or may not have had validity. The consideration of this and the lipstick tube found at the site of the murder did indicate one thing for certain. The case with Abby inscribed on it, did have a significant correlation in this mystery, and surely both were connected with the case.

Kara and Bruce, both, knew what had to be done next. They would have to report their findings to the police, even though their faith in the police was not the greatest. So, with that, they then took pictures of the case and documented the facts as brought to light by Matt and their own suppositions. Then, this too was put away In the safe place, Kara had designated as a good hiding place for the photos of the clues and the other analyses of the case. Their next move would be to provide the police, the Chief, with what they had discovered. After all, they had more manpower and a system for solving this type thing.

But, on their way to the police station, another clue, which Bruce found on his windshield, became evident. It was a note of cutout letters from a newspaper, spelling out the words BACK OFF OR ELSE. This made it obvious, someone did not want them investigating and having any more involvement in the case. Maybe, the murderer or murderers were getting nervous and were trying to scare them out of it. No matter, whatever was going on meant that they were getting closer, and someone was worried. Kara took a photo of the warning note and said "We need to get to the police, now." Bruce agreed and they jumped in Bruce's car and were at the station in a matter of minutes.

Upon arriving, Bruce asked the policeman manning the front desk, "Could we talk to the Chief?"

"Who do I say wants to see him?" replies the policeman. Kara spoke up, "Kara Steele and Bruce Stanton. We have information on the Beth Reeves case." The policeman picked up a phone and forwarded the message to the Chief and then said, "Go on in, you know where it is don't you?" Kara nodded a yes, and she and Bruce started toward the Chief's office. Kara knocked at the door and was waived in by the Chief, who said, "What can I do for you two, and it had better be good." Kara's dislike for this man continued to be apparent, as she responded, "We have some things, to do with Beth Reeve's case, you might be interested in. Do you want the long story or the short story?" It's getting to be time for my break, and I'm looking forward to my doughnut and coffee, so let's have the short story to start." He replies. Kara states, "Here it is, I went back to the park and found this case for cosmetics, with the name Abby on it, which I believe is connected to the lipstick tube, which I believe, may have been the murder weapon, having an undetectable poison on it, which

Beth used. Now, since then, Bruce and I have had a warning in the form of a threat to stay out of it, so I believe we are close." She then lays the case and the note on the desk of the Chief, who responds with, "That's all good, but how do I know, you didn't manufacture this stuff and your idea of how it was done, just to throw me off your own suspicious trails? Do you have any other proof of your own innocence or anything more concrete, than what you have given me?" Kara and Bruce look at each other in amazement, and finally stare at the Chief and Kara says, "You are really a character, aren't you? We are trying to clear our names by doing your work for you, and all you can do is say is your suspicions, no proof, just suspicions, that we may be involved in the murder. You're supposed take the clues and weigh the facts and come to a good conclusion about the case. Are you a hypocrite posing as a Chief of Police, or what?" And with that, Kara and Bruce storm out of the office.

Back on the street, Bruce looks at Kara, who is still steaming mad, and says, "Can you imagine the gall of that guy? Here we are helping, and he accuses us again, of having something to do with a murder." Kara nods yes and says, "He is either an imbecile or he wants us to continue doing his work for him by attacking our integrity, so we can prove him wrong. Either way, it looks as if, we are still on the hook and need to sort things out and give him his killer." Bruce asked Kara, "What do we do now?" Kara replies with, "Well the Chief is no help, and I'm ready to get free from any suspicion or connection. I say we meet with Matt again, and we start from square one to go over everything, we have, and do some soul searching to see if we missed anything. What about you, what are your thoughts?" Bruce immediately answers, "That sounds like a plan. But, I have some work to do. You know, I still need to pay the bills. You and Matt can look it over a couple of days or so, and you can fill me in later." "Ok" says Kara.

So, Matt and Kara, get together at the Library and begin going over the photos of the clues and the documented stuff, including suspicions, conjectures, and any kind of ideas of how they may have missed something. As they had everything sprawled out on Matt's desk for review, Ms. Abbott interrupted saying, "Excuse me, but I have a new shipment of about 48 books to authenticate and locate in their proper places. But, I see you have something else going on, so I could come back later." She happens to glance at the photos and pauses briefly, with a query, she asks, "Do these have something to do with Mrs. Reeves' demise? I just noticed something pertaining to the photos, the coin in the photo was in Mrs. Reeves' possession before she met her end. She had brought the coin into the Library and was inquiring about a book on the myths surrounding ancient coins. She had said that she was determining value." Kara replies, "That's very interesting. Did she have any kind of item she was carrying the coin in, or did you notice a case of any kind?" Ms. Abbott replies, "No, I didn't notice anything in particular. Why, is that important? I remember Mr. Reeves mentioning that you had given the police a number of clues to help their investigation, but I didn't know the specifics on any of them." Kara says, "Well, we don't know, but a cosmetic case was found near the scene of the crime in the park. And, we need to confirm or eliminate the case as a clue." "Let me take a look. Maybe Mrs. Reeves had brought it in at another time." Matt reached over to pick up the photo of the cosmetic case with the name Abby inscribed on it and gave it to the elderly librarian, who looked at the photo and immediately gave it back to Matt, saying, "No, I don't recognize it." Kara says, "Are you sure? This is very important. I'm certain, the case has something to do with the crime against Beth or Mrs. Reeves, as you call her. Do you, by the way, have any knowledge of anyone who may have rented books, or anyone you may have met in town named Abby?" She says quickly, sensing the importance, "Well, there are a couple of women, who have rented books here at the Library, before with that name, but, I've never seen them with that particular case, or have any notion of them doing such a thing as killing someone, and for what reason would they want to kill Mrs. Reeves? But, that brings to mind, I did see Mrs. Reeves with a woman, that I didn't know or recognize, and she had me get the same book about the Myths associated with these coins, that she had looked at before. I didn't think anything of it until just now. The woman was obviously a foreigner, by the way she spoke and dressed. " Matt looked at Ms. Abbott and released her saying, "That will be all for now, thank you. And, maybe we can help you with those books in a few minutes, ok?" She nods as understanding and exits.

The rest of the morning was taken up with more questions than answers. Matt and Kara did help Ms. Abbott with the working up the books, and after finishing, Matt suggests, "We should all go to the Diner for a sandwich or pizza. How about it ladies?" Ms. Abbott abruptly says she can't due to she has another appointment at noon. But, Kara nods her head as a yes, and the three close the Library for lunch and go their respective ways.

With this new information and recollection of the clues and where they were found, Kara and Matt try to configure how this new piece of information from Ms. Abbott, regarding the foreign woman with Beth at the Library, could be relative to the case. This foreign mystery woman could be Abby or not, and what about the coin. It must play a part in all this.

"All this thinking has made me hungry," says Matt, as their food is delivered to their table. Kara agrees and begins eating her personal pizza. Matt has a ham sandwich and fries, and they both eat as if they had missed breakfast. But, while eating, Kara asked Matt, "You don't remember anything about this mystery woman, huh?" He replies, "No, and this is the first I've even heard about it. Do you think it could tie in with the Emporium and, say, some kind of dealings they may have had with Beth over the coin? After all, that coin is worth a lot of money, enough to kill for, I'd say. And, if I may ask, where are the police with their case solving, anyhow?" Kara immediately replies, "I don't know, but let's give them a call." And, she picks up the phone to call the Chief's office and says, "This is Kara Steele. Could I please speak with the Chief of Police regarding the demise of Beth Reeves?" The voice at the other end states, "Yes, I'll put you through to him." In a matter of a minute or so, the Chief says, " Hello Ms. Steele and what can I do for you?" She replies, "Matt Reeves and I, who you say are still suspects in Beth's murder, were wandering if there were any new circumstances in the case, which could clear our names. Do you have any news for us?" The Chief was quiet for a moment and then said, "We are pursuing some other paths and clues. I know you were at the Park the other day, did you find anything new? Maybe, we could share a little more Information with each other." Kara hesitated and replies, "I saw some things, but I'm uncertain if there is a direct connection with the case. But, if you tell me what you are pursuing, maybe these things relate somehow. So, why don't you fill me in first?" The Chief responds with, "Well to begin with, we have come across two other persons of interest, and our FBI agent is looking into the background of that Emporium, you had spoken of earlier. One of the persons of interest was a foreign person of shady character, who was seen outside Mrs. Reeves' office a couple of times before the murder. He had black snake tattoos on his neck and arms, per a couple of witnesses, who saw him sitting outside the shop, just watching." "Is there any sort of connection with any women in your investigation or the FBI agent's investigation to this point?" Kara asks. The Chief replies with, "You are still a suspect, and there is a woman from the Emporium, who could have had motive and opportunity to kill Mrs. Reeves, the same as you. Why, do you still believe those old clues from the Park could pertain to the case, with all the people, who visit the park daily? What could make you feel as if these so called clues will be pertinent to the case?" Kara realizes at this point, that the Chief has tunnel vision and is not open to different perceptions, probably, especially from her. "So, you don't think of those findings at the Park as being relative? I believe you are already convinced, I had something to do with this case, and you are too stubborn or just pig headed, to not follow any other clues that are staring you in the face!" She responded. "Well, another way of looking at this, is you and your friends could be trying to derail the investigation with these so called findings in the Park. Maybe, you're trying to buy time or hope someone else will be the fall guy for this murder and then you could be in the clear." Says the Chief. Kara immediately states, "That's ridiculous, and yes, I know someone else did this, because my friends and I, as you say, didn't have any wrong doing in this deadly act. And, I resent the fact that you are still worrying about me and my friends, instead of finding the real killer or killers. I was about to tell you of another possible clue, but you are not listening, anyhow, are you? You have a one track mind, when it comes to me, so why should I waste my breath?" The Chief replies, "You know you are obligated to turn over anything you might find that may or may not be related to this case, don't you?" Kara, somewhat irate, says, "Oh, I will share with you anything I find, but I will be making photos and documentation regarding anything, I find, and I will be keeping track of everything in my own defense, since you are so hell bent on trying to blame me and my friends, as you put it."

CHAPTER 10

Made To Order

As Kara returns the phone to the off position, she exclaims, "He thinks, we are the only real suspects in this case! He has made it clear as to who he believes the culprits who killed Beth are. He still believes we are more than employer and employee or just friends. The only logical thing to do is to solve this mystery on our own, which means we will have to put our heads together, you, me, and Bruce, and try to come up with a suspect or suspects, so we can finally try to close in on the real murderer or murderers." Matt agrees, and says, "We need to call Bruce right now, and then we could set a time for all three of us to go over all the clues, again, and start naming some likely suspects for investigation, either near or afar." "I agree. We can meet at Beth's office again, and maybe, something will be outstanding enough as to be a way of determining something else to go on. We have clues, but nothing about any of the clues, we've found, jumps out at me." Kara replies.

And, so it was determined that the three, still suspects, would meet at Beth's business office to go over everything again in hopes of finding something more definite to go on. Upon arrival at the office, the three greet one another, as Matt unlocks the door to the antique or collectible business, he states this. "We can begin by going through the old files of customers again in search of something. But, then again, I don't know what we're looking for. Do you?" Kara, says, "We are looking for anything pertinent to the clues we have discovered and anything that is out of the ordinary, no matter what." Bruce says, "We should find documentation on some of this stuff, such as on the coin, or maybe a name that seems related to something else, like the Emporium, who did business with Beth. There may be others we didn't pick up on before. Let's get to looking."

While going through Beth's files and searching for any evidence, there was talk about how it came about that these three were suspects. Matt was first to say, "Well, you have to admit the town is small, and there's a lot of gossip about anyone or anything that can be talked about. For instance, Kara was looking for a job and needing to meet the people she would be in contact with at the Library, so, "to get two birds with one stone", I arranged, admittedly for personal reasons as well, to have meetings with Kara at restaurants and have her at social gatherings, and I also wanted to be in contact with her at work, so the word on the street, would be that we were suspicions of us being more than employer and employee. I did kind of get her into this situation." Kara then states, "Well, that may well be but, I went along with the deception, knowing it was to try to help save your marriage, and, besides I was new in town and it was somewhat fun. Bruce became involved when he began fraternizing with me, and this could have been problematic due to both of us." Bruce chimed in, "Yea, we were all sort of pulled into the mix of it. But, Beth's murder is what really brought about our problems." Kara says, "I don't really blame the Chief for considering us suspects, due to it all sort of pointed to us. The gossip, the dates with Matt, then Bruce's appearance on the scene, right at the time of Beth's demise. It's as if we were all just casts as the culprits. But, that is even more reason to find something, anything that we can tie to Beth's murderer or murderers to, so as to clear us." During this time of talk, Kara, Matt, and Bruce were scouring the office for any kind of clue to help them point a finger at the real criminal. They had been at it for two to three ours, and just as they were about to give up, Matt interjects with, "There seems to be a loose board behind the desk that I hadn't noticed before." As Matt pries the board away from the wall a bit, he notices a small book of sorts within, and he reaches in to retrieve it. Suddenly, Kara exclaims. "What is it? What does it say?" While Matt begins reading and thumbing through the pages. Amazed, Matt says to Kara, "Here, have a look for yourself." And, he falls back into the chair. Kara took the book, which appeared to be a small diary or something such as this, and began reading and looking through the book, as Bruce leaned over her shoulder, also reading. In the first pages of the book were, what appeared to be, Beth's confessions. She had written about illicit affairs she had been a party to. Both adulterous and some criminal affairs, such as, "went to bed with a business acquaintance by the name of a John Hernton two days before the 4th of July" and "though I am making money, it's not enough, I'm still searching" and "the markup on these Black Market items is tremendous" entered only weeks before Beth's death, made up the composition of the book. The book was small, but it had a lot of information and names of her extramarital partners and her crime based contacts. There were enough suspects and damning topics with dates to raise suspicion onto any number of these people pointed out in the book. At last, there were others on the suspect list, and the three who found this could be taken off the list. "At last, we will no longer be suspects of Beth's murder, surely." States Bruce. They all sit and become almost in a trance, as they consider what's been found. After a while, about 20 minutes or so, Kara, still seated with the book in hand, says, "No, I believe we are still on the hook as suspects, and maybe even more than before. Can you see, if we take this to the Chief, he will look at it as more damning evidence against us. He will think Matt knew of all this, and he conspired with me and Bruce to kill Beth, because of our association and friendship with each other. Also, since Bruce and I are somewhat new in town, what better murder suspects than strangers, who happened to be together at the time of the murder? He may even be thinking of us as hitmen or something. No, we could have been cleared as suspects a long time ago, if the Chief wasn't so narrow minded. And, also, if we turn this book over to the law now, the real killer might escape, if this comes out. I think our best bet is to continue our search on the sly, without the Chief or his so-called help. Anyway, with us still suspects in everyone's mind, the real killer feels safe. Do you agree?" Both the men nod their heads as to say yes and keep looking for more information or clues.

After a few hours of searching and sifting to no better results, the group decided to call it an evening and left locking the door behind them. After some much needed rest, Kara awoke the next morning to the phone ringing. She climbed from bed and quickly answered the phone with "Hello. May I ask who is calling?" The voice on the other end of the phone call was a woman's, a voice that Kara didn't recognize. She asked again, "What did you say your name was?" Just then the call was ended by the mysterious woman. She had told Kara to be very cautious about her snooping into the matters of Beth Reeves' business and hung up. She began to dial Matt's phone number to ask him if he had a call, too. Upon hearing his phone ringing, Matt answered, "Hello." "Did you get a threatening phone call recently, regarding Beth's business dealings?" Asked Kara. Matt, at the other end of the call says. "No, but I have had a feeling, as if someone was watching me." Kara replies, "I believe we all have those feelings. Well, I just had a call from a woman, I could make out who she was, telling me to back off. We either are getting close, or some people are getting very nervous, because they believe we are close to finding something." "I believe I'll call Bruce and see if he has heard anymore." Kara states. When she does call Bruce, he is adamant that he hasn't heard anything, and nor has he seen any women in town other than the usual people, he sees in his routine. But, he does say "What about the people at the Emporium? Were there any women involved with them that we know of?" "It makes sense. That's how she got my number. It must have been from the Crime Lab, when we were investigating the coin. I'm sure that is what they want, and they don't want us butting in on anything they're connected to, such as their dealings with Beth." Kara says. Bruce agrees, "They must be the ones, I have felt watching me. I thought it might be the Chief's men, but with all that's going on, we can't rule out the idea of someone from out of town being involved." "That's true. The killer or killers could be from anywhere, so let's not forget about these people either." Kara says. She went on to say, "I believe it is time to do some research on those people at the Emporium, if nothing more than to eliminate them as suspects to the murder." Bruce says, "Leave it to me. I know how to get some information about them." And with that, the two hung up the phones to get on with what they intended to do.

Kara, after some coffee and pastry, decided to wade into the evidence box again. She began by looking at the things which she considered most significant with the case. She pulled up the pictures of the coin, the copies of the lab report and the cost estimate of the coin, along with the coin purse inscribed with Abby on it, and finally the small diary type book, which Beth kept for whatever reason. The book could have other directions to aim at. And if only, Kara knew why Beth kept such a book hidden away. For instance, the coin purse could have been dropped by a jealous wife or lover, which would eliminate the coin's significance, unless the coin was in the purse and both were lost at the scene. The book could have an Abby or an Abbigail written in it somewhere, or could have a lover of Abby's, which would make sense. She began looking through the diary book, and she was looking for any clue as to who could have been involved in the murder or had anything to do with the coin, so as to find its meaning or information regarding it. As she read on, it wasn't until near the last posting in the book, that she noticed something that caught her eye. Beth had written, "Finally, Matt is starting to see how it is. He is dating some new person in town. I was wandering when he would try to get revenge on me, or at least see how it really is." Kara thought to herself, "This would definitely hurt Matt and me, if the Chief read it. We undoubtedly, would be number one on his suspect list, if we weren't already." Yes, Beth was a bad one, but Matt still loved her in a way to try to salvage the marriage. That's what made Kara a suspect in all of this, trying to help. As Kara continued reading, she noted some appointments, Beth had made, on the day of her demise. A couple of them stood out. One was with a woman with only the name Sylvia, and it was followed by the phone number which matched the one Kara had used to call the Emporium a while back. The time of the appointment was 5:00. The other had only one letter, A, and had only a time of 5:30 on the day of Beth's end. So, the mystery is now becoming more distinct. These were two people who were to meet with Beth on the day of her murder. These women could only have been after the coin, a valuable collectible which is surely related to the coin purse with Abby on it, and the Emporium, which we know wanted the coin from the start. But, how would Kara, Matt, and Bruce find these people? Kara decided to see if either of the guys had come across anything yet. She continued to look through the book until she saw something else which caught her attention. In the footnotes on the same page as the appointments was found this message to Beth, herself, "Three possible buyers for coin, still need to get bids." Kara thought to herself, "A third possibility as suspects."

She continued to read to see if there was any indication of who this third person might be. The diary did not state any other possible name but, in a notation on a previous page, a short sentence written by Beth stated, "This guy sure does have a hoarse voice, enough to scare me." As she read the book, Kara noticed another peculiar thing which was noted by Beth on the day she lost her life. The notation read like this, "I saw a grouping of crows outside my window, today, not just black birds, but crows." Kara instantly knew what this meant. It was an omen. And as it happened this had come true for Beth. Kara thought to herself, "I'd bet Beth was worried and reluctant to meet with these two appointments that day, because apparently, she knew the meaning of the grouping of crows." Kara decided to put the book in a safe place and get ready for the day. She needed to talk with Bruce and Matt as soon as possible, about what she had found.

Upon leaving her apartment, Kara had stuck the book, or diary, whatever it was, in her purse and proceeded to go to Bruce's place as to show him what she had learned. As she left the building, she noticed a car parked down from her apartment building. The driver was laid back and resting," possibly asleep", she thought. Kara decided to walk by the automobile and get a better look at this person, who was obviously here to keep an eye on her or someone. As she passed by the auto with the this person in it, she noticed a snake tattoo on the man's neck, and she could tell he was an outsider due to his clothes and skin head and earring. He was most definitely from out of town. With this, she crossed the street and headed for Bruce's. Kara reached Bruce's office within a few minutes, and found him with customers, so she decided to find a chair and have a seat. Bruce saw her and nodded with recognition. Approximately fifteen minutes passed, and Bruce handed some forms to the customers, and then he walked with them to the door. After he closed the door behind them, Bruce looked at Kara and asked, "Did you find anything new?" And, immediately in reply, Kara says, "I located Beth's diary and some very important information in it. Some of it leads a reader to believe Matt and I were having an affair. And with all that was happening then, it certainly looked as if we were "Made to Order" for this murder." She then pointed out the notation Beth had made about Matt finding another woman and having an affair. She continued, "You can see where all the implications are directed toward me and Matt, as being lovers, and therefore having the motive to kill her." Kara, began looking through the book and found excerpts regarding the appointments Beth had made for that day of her end. She spoke, "You can see, she had appointments with at least two people that day at the park. And, I believe a woman had something to do with her demise, or it was a woman who killed her. What do you think, after reexamining the clues and the notations in this book? Do you think we are on the right track, or what?" Bruce sat at his desk just then and began making a list of sorts. He replied, "Yes, and if you try to set a scenario for what happened, this all falls into line with what we have believed all along. The collectable coin, the lipstick tube, the small purse of sorts, and finally the threatening call from a woman, definitely means a woman was at the scene with Beth when she died. There may have been others, but a woman was there." "How are you doing in running down some names of potential suspects?" Kara asked. Bruce replied, "Not so good. All I have to go on are the same names, we have had for a while. But, I am going to place a few phone calls today to different places, such as the Police Station, The Emporium, and maybe Matt could recall a couple of people who could be involved. I know he hasn't had any thoughts as to who could have done this, but he may know of someone in their circle of friends we haven't touched on yet." "Let me talk with Matt. I need to go by the Library anyhow, to return a book." Kara says. With that she turned to leave, when Bruce says, "Are we having dinner tonight at Mitchell's?" Kara nodded and says, "Seven o'clock is fine. Pick me up, alright?" Bruce nods an affirmative gesture.

As Kara is walking away from The Real Estate Office, she notices the man with the snake tattoo sitting across the street from the office. Not even giving it another thought, she decided to ask the man a few questions. As she approached the man's car, he started looking away from her toward a different direction. She moved slowly, toward the car's driver's side and casually asked the man, "Could you tell me where the Park is?" The man didn't respond, he simply gazed at her in a kind of disbelief. She asked, "I'm to meet someone at the Park, and I'm not certain which way to go. Do you live around here?" The man looked downward saying, "I'm new in town, and I'm not certain but, I believe the Park is that way." As he pointed to a nearby street. Kara quickly states, "Well, I have to meet a friend, Abby, within an hour." She looks at him to see his response. He barely moves, only fidgets a bit in his seat. Then he says, "Sorry, Lady, that's all I can tell you."

And then he starts the vehicle and begins to drive away. Kara has the forethought to read his license plate, and then she writes it down on a piece of paper, along with the color and make of the car. With that, she starts down the street toward the Library, where she can return the book, check on things, and talk with Matt. Upon arrival at the Library, she says hello to Ms. Abbott, who was busy cataloguing some books and getting them ready to put away. The kindly old librarian responds with, "Hello dear. Are you here for work or pleasure, today?" Kara replies, "I'm here to return a book and speak with Matt, I mean, Mr. Reeves. But, I'm hoping within the next week or two, I can get back to work, and I can help you with doing our jobs, as you have been so kind to do for me in my absence." Ms. Abbott responds with, "Think nothing of it. I'm glad to help in any way I can." Kara turned to go visit with Matt, but remembered she hadn't returned the book yet. She stopped by the check-in desk, where she noted on the register, the time and date her book was returned. She then ambled toward the many aisles of bookshelves and found where her book should go. In doing this, she noticed another book beside hers, the title being "A Drug to Kill By" by an unknown author. Curious, she picked up the book and began thumbing through the pages. She came across numerous listings of drugs found at both drugstores or on the street, which could be used in killing anything from pests to animals, or could be used against humans. She wandered why she hadn't seen this book earlier, when she had checked out her book on different drugs. She went back to the register, but no listing of this particular book was in it. Obviously, someone had taken the book without checking it out, and then replaced it in its proper place. The question was who. It wouldn't do any good to ask, because anyone could have added to some other books, and thereby carried it out unnoticed. Kara started toward Matt's office, wandering if the mystery woman was living amongst them or from out of town. Matt saw Kara coming and said. "Come in and take a seat. I know why you're here. I spoke with Bruce a short while ago. Something about Beth's diary, I believe." Kara answered with "Yes, but, as I was leaving Bruce's office, I noticed the man who had been following me, and I stopped and asked him a few questions. Anyhow, I decided that he could be a part of this mystery. I'm just not certain how yet." Matt looked at her a little stunned and spoke, "You shouldn't go so far as to approach a suspect alone. It could be very dangerous, especially, if you do run across the killer or killers. You should wait for me or Bruce to be with you." The two sat and talked a while, about the diary and information Kara had found, and how it may be important to the case. She also reminded him of the dinner that night with her and Bruce. And, she told Matt about Bruce's making phone calls to try to get some information on some leads for suspects. And, finally, Kara rose to leave and turned to say to Matt, "We're going to sort this mess out, be sure of that. See you tonight." With that being said, Kara left the Library and started home to get ready for dinner and to gather her thoughts.

At five minutes of seven o'clock, Kara heard a horn honking outside her building and peered out the window to see Bruce waiting for her. She thought to herself, "This is what you have when you're going steady, a man honking for you instead of coming to the door. Oh well, it works for me." And she hurried out the door to meet him. Kara opens the door of Bruce's car and jumps in, saying, "Are we in a hurry?" Bruce replies, "The reservation is at 7:10, and we don't want to be late." The Corvette cruised down the street and made its way to Mitchell's. The restaurant was packed with only a few vacant tables. Upon entering, Bruce says to the attendant at the front desk, "Table for three." And the attendant reached for three menus and said, "Follow me, please." The table was near a bar and not too far from the restrooms. And, it seems these are the two things you look for when going into a restaurant. It seems so.

Kara and Bruce scanned the menus, while talking in a low tone of the case they were involved with. Bruce asked, "I know we have more information, but are we any closer to finding who did the murder? I have made some phone calls, and I came up with a couple of names associated with the Emporium, but they may only be middlemen." Kara then asked, "What are they and can you describe these two?" "The man's name is Aaron, and he is the same one we saw earlier, when we retrieved the coin, remember? And the woman's name is Golda, and I'm not certain of what she looks like." Kara nods and replies, "I have a license number and description of someone who has been following me. He and I had a few words when I left your place today. I need you to find out as much as you can about him. Who he works for, where he's from, stuff like that." She then handed Bruce the paper with the car description and license number on it. About this time, Matt comes in, sees them, and he hurriedly moves toward their table. Upon arriving, he says a greeting and starts talking, "I hope you two are doing well. I just had a call from the police, asking me if we had found any new evidence at Beth's office the other night." Bruce asked, "What did you tell them?" "I told them, not yet, but we would be looking in her office again. I felt, I had to say something to keep them satisfied." Then Matt grabbed a chair and sat down at the table. Kara started the conversation, "We have a number of clues to this mystery, but we haven't tied them together, yet. Any ideas?" Both men looked at her, and finally Bruce said, "My bet is on the people at the Emporium. They have the most to gain and they fit the type who would do this. And, the woman in the group is a from a foreign background. And her name happens to be Abiyan, a Hindu name, I believe. The males also have foreign backgrounds and are here as Indian citizens attempting to become US citizens. I had to search through government census files, public, of course and some googling of the business and its owners to locate information on them. Anyhow, they are my best bet, as I said." Matt, taking this all in, speaks up saying, "They have been high on the list ever since we began this investigation, if that's what you want to call it. Now, do we want to share with the police or what? Maybe hire a professional private investigator, or what is your suggestion?" The waitress comes round at this time to ask if the three are ready to order and to fill their water glasses. Kara looks at her and begins ordering her salad and shrimp, while the guys both put in orders for steak and potato. As the waitress takes the orders and turns to leave, Kara leans over the table to softly speak to the guys, saying, "We have to do this ourselves, because we are high on the Chief's list of suspects, so going to the police won't do. As for hiring a private eye, that may not be such a bad idea. Does anyone have a suggestion on who we might get?" There's a moment of silence, and then Bruce says, "There is a fellow in Chaffee, who may be able to do what we need. All we need is for him to follow these people and/or get more information on them, to see if they are that heavily involved as to murder someone, correct?" Matt inquires, "What is his name? And, what do you feel he will charge, since we already have a great deal of evidence or clues, whatever?" Kara, answers with, "Well, even if we hire someone to follow those people and investigate them, I'm not quitting on this case. I want my name taken off the suspect list. I'm getting very tired of being followed and hounded by the police and God knows who else." The waitress interrupts the discussion with the orders to be served, salads only, and then turns to go. Then, Bruce speaks up, "You know, I believe that PI is named O'Brian and I'll have to call him to see what he will do and how much money he'll charge." Kara, says in between bites, "Well, I'm going to continue following the clues and the money, since the coin was worth as much as it is. And, there's bound to be something turn up pretty soon. The guy following me and the police are becoming more brazen and apparent in what they're doing. I don't know about you two, but I'm getting very irritated by all this."

After dinner, Matt headed home, while Kara and Bruce went to Kara's place to have a drink and loosen up a little. Upon arriving at Kara's, Matt began making a couple of drinks, a Jack and coke for him and a rum and coke for Kara. As the two sat and talked about everything which had brought them to this point, the subject of tying the knot came up. "Have you thought about remarrying someone?" Asked Bruce. "Not much. I feel it's too soon after my last marriage ended for me to give it much thought. To tell you the truth, I really didn't have any ideas on being with anyone again." She replies. Bruce says, "Well, I have had many relationships with many women, and this is as close as I have come to even thinking of marriage. Maybe, it's the age, or maybe I believe, I may have found the right woman." "I feel very good about you, too, and possibly, I may be in love with you. But, I have to think of all these problems and incidents associated with the murder, that I have to clear up or at least try to solve as to relieve my own predicament." Kara responds. "I'm on the suspect list as well, and I still have feelings, and I need to live my life, just as you do. But, I don't want the situation dictating my every thought or my plans on how to live my life." Bruce states. The two finish their drinks, and begin to feel like the evening is drawing to a close. Bruce stands and says, "I had better leave. I have things to do tomorrow, and I still want to run a search on any person or persons with the name Abigale or Abbey, who may be connected with the purse, you found. I can stop by City Hall and check their records first." Kara replies, "Alright, but I don't think our conversation is over, only postponed till a later date. Is that ok with you?" Bruce nods his head to say yes, and as he opens the door to go, he says, "I'll also call that fellow O'Brian. We are going to clear up this mess one way or another, I'm certain of it." As he walks out the door to leave, Kara feels more optimistic than before, and she now knows, they have a plan that could lead to the answer to this whole mystery of Beth's death. She feels the clues will lead to the killer or killers.

The next morning, Kara went to her special safe place, where the clues, the three of them have collected and kept, are stored and began going over every last one, and she tried to put them in a coordinated time sequence as related to the murder, as best she could, anyhow. "It was like a jigsaw puzzle with some of the pieces missing." She thought. As she finished her coffee, Kara decided to go out for a sandwich, before heading for the Library. She walked down street toward the small diner, she frequented when she first moved to Rossville. The people there hadn't changed much, although there was more of a hushed conversation by all, as she entered and found a table. The women, she had met when first she moved here, didn't dare approach her now, since she was thought of as a murderer or accomplice, at this point. Kara ordered a breakfast sandwich and a cup of coffee and said to the waitress, "Could I have a few of those doughnuts to go, please, including my sandwich?" The waitress nodded and walked off, not saying a word. Her coffee was hot and black and tasted good as she drank it to the last drop at just the time her order to go arrived. Kara paid her waitress and started out the door to the street. It was only a short distance to the Library, where Kara found her way inside and walked up to the front desk with a bag in hand. "Ms. Abbott, how are you?" she asked and drew a doughnut from the bag to give to her. The elderly librarian paused, took the doughnut, and said, "Well, and thank you for the pastry. I suppose you will be looking for Mr. Reeves?"

Kara gazed toward Matt's office and said, "Yes, I need to speak with him." The spinster pointed and said, "I'll call him and tell him you're here."

"After I speak with Mr. Reeves, I thought I would try to catch up on some work. You haven't completed all my work for me, have you?" asked Kara. The small framed elderly lady looked up at Kara, and said, "I haven't done all that was assigned to you, if that's what you mean. But, I have completed some things. You can see for yourself, when you are ready. And, by the way, everyone in town asks about your investigation of Mrs. Reeves' end. Do you have anything that will bring your, what seems to be an obsession, to a close?"

"Not yet, but we are getting closer to finding the killer or killers." States Kara. She continues by saying, "The police have their own search going on, and I'm confident someone will crack the case sooner or later. Suspects, other than Mr. Reeves, Bruce, and myself, are being considered, and some are prime suspects in my book. When the clues start coming more together, I'd bet there won't be any doubt as to who took Beth's life." With that, Kara started walking toward Matt's office, and upon reaching the door, she knocks a couple of soft knocks. Matt speaks up saying, "Come on in. What's on your mind today, Kara?" She replies with "I have some breakfast for you. And, I would like to do some work around here. I also, would like to do some more snooping with the books, to see what I can dig up." "What kind of books?" He asked. Books which could reinforce the information I now have on the time it takes to poison someone with an oral concoction. I still believe our original clues, such as the lipstick tube, coin, and other items found at the Park, are the deal breakers for solving this thing." She continues by saying "We're overlooking something, though. Maybe, the method or time or culprit, or maybe all of the above. In other words, something is missing. I think it has to do with motive. The coin could have been motive, jealousy or rage over an affair, or maybe another reason. But, one thing is certain, it was premeditated and it was carried out with a type of vengeance toward Beth, due to the type of murder, and you may have been involved in this so called vengeance, somehow, sort of unknowingly." After listening to this, Matt says, "Then, it could have been due to a business dealing, someone wanting vengeance, a jealous wife, a jilted lover, or someone Beth hurt very badly in the past. How will we be able to come to a conclusion with the clues, we have?" "The answer is there, but we don't have the missing pieces yet. But, we will, and I'm hoping it will be soon. We are getting close. Time to hit the books, so to speak." States Kara as she opens the door to leave Matt's office. Kara moves toward the Library's many aisles of books and looking at the exact row she needs, she begins searching through the titles, until a certain title jumps out at her, "A Toxic Solution", a book about a Black Widow killer, who used poison as a means to an end. And since it was a true story, the facts within might be more applicable to the case than her own hypotheses. Kara began reading the case study of the murderess and found some similarities with Beth's murder. After all, Kara had believed the killer to be a woman from early on. As she read on in the book of the Black Widow, she found that only after several murders, did the killer make enough mistakes to finally realize who she was. Due to the clues or errors the killer made, a clearer direction to the killer was determined. The book was not long and entailed, and she was able to read it in a couple of hours. Anyhow, she had gotten what she was looking for from the book. Finally, she laid the book down and began doing some work. There was not so much, since her co-worker had done a lot of it. At the end of the day, Kara had come a little closer to figuring out that the missing pieces to the puzzle would probably not be located, unless the killer was very careless, and Kara wasn't going to count on that as a possibility. She picked up her things and now that she had the book to show the guys and the Chief, she felt somewhat reassured, and left the Library.

Kara was back at her apartment now, and she needed to look at some of the clues a little closer now. She went to her safe place, and she picked up the notebook diary, the purse with Abby monogramed on it, and she needed to look at the evidence sheet concerning the lipstick tube. After a lengthy examination of the three items, Kara noted these all had to be tied together. The notebook indicated the time and place, the purse indicated where the killer laid in wait for the victim in an area beside the bench, and the tube of lipstick could only have been the murder weapon, in this case. This had to be true, since no other scenario would fit here. But, the motive and suspect were still elusive in trying to fit the pieces all together. Kara still needed more to give her suspicions any sort of credibility. It's been a month or more into this investigation, and the Chief is still not any help. Kara will have to rely on any or all information Bruce can add, or Matt may have forgotten something which could shed some light on a suspect. "If we had a suspect, we could figure out the motive, or if we had a distinct motive, we could possibly come up with a suspect." She thought to herself. In the book, she had just read about how the investigators and criminologists involved in solving the case, the evidence was hashed over and rehashed over, time and time again, in efforts to fill in the missing pieces to a puzzle, and she felt this is what she and the guys would have to do to ever realize what they needed. "And, also, what about the private detective? Is that a waste or could he shine a light on something?" She was thinking to herself. Kara began thinking of just how she had gotten involved with this mystery, all the way from the proposed charade Matt and she played a part in to make Beth jealous, which as she thinks back now, was a mistake on her part, but, at the time it was the only way to get the job at the Library. She thought about the Chief's apparent lack of forethought on who might really be a suspect in the case, and finally, she thought about all which has happened, not only with the case, but with Bruce, who she is very interested in romantically. And, this leads her to now, and what is going to happen next. "What's her next step, and what is going to become of all of us?" she thought. Well after a short nap, Kara decided to call Bruce. She dialed his number and waited for a response. "Hello, is this Kara?" Bruce said at the other end of the call. Kara says, "Yes, and I was just now thinking about you, and how we have come very close do to the onset of Beth's ending. I need you to come over tonight, and I'll fix a snack and we could have a couple of drinks or something, and we could go over the clues again. How do you feel about that?" Bruce replies, "That will be fine. I'll bring some cheese and a bottle of wine."

When Bruce arrives at Kara's and knocks on the door, he is thinking kind thoughts of this woman that he has come to know. Kara opens the door and immediately took the bag of wine and cheese and put it in the refrigerator. "Are you hungry now, or would you like to wait? All we are having is some soup and some luncheon sandwiches. And, then we will tackle your cheese and wine. Does this sound alright?" Kara asked. Bruce nodded with approval and said, "I'm ready now. I'm famished." The two began eating their meal while talking about the day they had. "Bruce, I believe we can get through this murder mystery case, but I have been wandering what will happen to us beyond the investigation. What will we do then?" Kara states. Bruce replies with, "We will be an item, you and me. We'll be together and not let life keep us apart." With this said, the two moved from the dinner table to the couch, where Kara began loosening Bruce's shirt and belt. Before long, the two lovers became entwined with each other in an embrace, while making love. Afterward, while getting dressed again, Bruce says with a smile, "Can we have some wine and cheese, now?" Kara, laughingly says, "Let's go." And they walk back to the kitchen to retrieve the goodies. During their late night snack, the two begin to discuss the case again, and Kara has told Bruce about the book she found, and the fact that some women can kill with a different type of motivation. She goes on to say, "The book has a similar motivation and results are the same as with Beth's end, if we think the motivation is money or in this case a valuable object. But, I've been thinking, what if money isn't the motivating factor, and love, jealousy, and revenge could be motivation here. What if we were even looking for the wrong type suspect, a jealous wife, a jilted lover, or someone who idolized Beth to the point of an unbalanced end is to be considered. This could happen, couldn't it?"

The next day started off slow, uneventful, until around 10:30 am, when the police station placed a call to Kara and then to Bruce and Matt, asking them to come downtown to the station at the Chief's request. Bruce had picked up Kara, and they were at the station in a matter of a few minutes, where they noticed Matt was already waiting to talk to the Chief. The three sat there for about 15 minutes, and then were brought back to the Chief's office. The Chief's first words were, "Well do you have anything for me? I know you've been doing some more snooping here and there. It doesn't matter. We, being the special agent from the FBI and I, have some news for you. You're no longer suspects. We have someone else who is good for this murder." Kara spoke up, "And who would that be, Chief?" He responds with, "Now, I can't reveal who he is at this time, but he is a vagrant who was seen near the park the evening of the murder." Bruce now speaks, "In other words, you feel the crime was not pre-meditated, but a random mugging?" Matt utters, "But, but." Before he could say anything more, the Chief interrupts saying, "He claims he's innocent, but we can place him at the scene that evening about 3:30 and he had a suspicious amount of cash on him, when we picked him up. And besides, he was spotted near the park around that time by an eye witness." Kara in a disbelieving tone asks,

"Is it possible that he had an accomplice? A female?" The Chief replies, "No, he is probably going down for this on his own. No one else is apparent for this, but him." Kara, again asks, "Can we go now?" The Chief opens the door and says, "Go ahead and go, but you all had better keep your noses clean after this."

With this, the group rose from their chairs and started toward the door. On the street, Matt said, "No female accomplice, and he believes a vagrant killed her, though she didn't have the markings of a mugging. What's up?" Kara says, "Yea, seems pretty fishy, as if they were trying to bait someone into thinking it's a done deal or something and lure them into a state of over confidence, so they would make the wrong move. I suppose he still believes we are good suspects, by him telling us about the vagrant." "Obviously, the police are not going to be of any help in finding the real killer or killers, since they're still fishing, or they have the wrong suspect In custody." Bruce states. Matt interjects, "Let's go have lunch and talk. We can take a different perspective now, since something is going on. Maybe, the true culprit will be flushed out into the open. Any way you look at it, finding Beth's killer is still left up to us, and I for one will not rest until my wife's killer or killers is or are brought to justice. So far, I've taken a back seat to solving this mystery, but we are getting so close and need to finish what we started." Bruce and Kara both looked at each other and then at Matt and Bruce says "We agree, and so, I've found some information on our friends at the Emporium. They were suspected of criminal activity in the past, according to old newspaper articles, which I found on the internet. It was theft and fraud, and they couldn't find enough evidence to convict, but this goes to show the type people they are. Whether they could kill to get what they want, that's another question for the police. Should we pass this information on to the police? Let them worry about these people, because they may be dangerous, or do we go after them with a little trap of sorts?" Kara responds, "We set a little trap. But, just not for them, but for anyone we can get to take the bait."

At lunch at the nearby diner, the group began again, after ordering, with another plan to draw out the killer or killers, whatever it might be. They sat at the back of the diner, so as not to be heard by anyone around and Kara brought out some paper and a pen. She starts with a few words to write an ad for the local paper. Found: A small purse with a girl's name starting with A embossed on it. To claim, come to the Library on Friday and describe. Bruce asks, "Are you sure you want them to meet you at the Library?" Kara says, "It's the only place I could think of that's public, and they wouldn't suspect anything." Bruce questions with, "What makes you think they will go after the bait?" She returns with, "I don't believe they will want a piece of evidence out there to be used to discover them if they are guilty, and a woman can't refuse an opportunity to get back something as personal as her clutch. Besides, it's not an admission of guilt to retrieve something you lost or was stolen. But, it would help to clear up some questions about this mysterious purse, we found at the Park. And to tell you the truth, it's all we have right now. I believe the purse and murder are connected. I believe the lipstick tube was used as a murder weapon, by administering poison to Beth. I didn't say anything before, because I wasn't sure, but now, this seems the only way she could have been killed. And I do believe she knew her attacker in some way."

The ad was to run three days, which seemed like an ample time for someone to respond to this Lost and Found purse, thought Kara. Finally, when Friday morning rolls around, of course Kara, Matt, and Bruce were curious as to if the ad worked. Now, Matt and Kara were at work this day, so as to be available, if and when someone came to answer the ad. Bruce was on call at his workplace and was waiting anxiously. The hours of the morning went by slowly with no one responding to the ad. After lunch and some small talk, Kara and Matt voiced a little concern as if no one would bite. Matt says, "Nothing yet, and I'm getting to think no one is going to show up." Kara agrees, "Yes, it looks as if either the owner didn't see the ad, or is not going to pick it up." They each went back to their work and tried to put the whole thing out of their minds. It was ten minutes to closing and Matt was getting ready to close the doors to the Library, Kara was getting ready to leave, and Ms. Abbott had just gone for the day, when a young woman in her early twenties came through the door and walked up to Kara to say "I have come about the purse." Kara, trying to hold back her excitement, says, "Do you believe the purse is yours?" "Yes, I can describe it to you. It is brown with the name Abby on it." The woman states. Kara responds with, "So, your name is Abby?" "Yes, Abby Monahyn." She says. "We need a little information, so we can release the purse back to you." Kara replies. "What's your age and a phone number in case there is a problem later?" Asked Kara. "Well, I didn't think you needed that, but I'm twenty-two and my phone number is 417-258-6723." After jotting down this prescribed information, Kara handed the clutch purse over to the young woman. The woman then turned and left the Library. Matt immediately asked, "Do you think that was wise, I mean giving her the purse? That was evidence." Kara replies, "Relax, I put a tiny minute transmitter in the lining of the purse. We can track it with a special App. for now, we need to close, and I need to get hold of Bruce." She then began dialing her phone for Bruce. He answers, "Hello, did someone come after the clutch?" Kara replied, "Yes, and I need you to rush over, so we can see where she goes." They each hung up the phone, and Bruce came directly to the Library to pick up Kara. Matt had decided to come along, and they sped off in the direction of the only bank in town, where the three could see the young woman entering. Since, this was a Friday, the bank was open to be available for their clientele who were just leaving work with their pay checks. They watched from across the street to see the woman leave about ten minutes later. They were ready to follow her, but the tracking device was not sending a signal of movement. The purse had to still be at the bank. A little confused the three sat in the car a few minutes to see if anyone would come to pick up the purse, which was obviously still inside. Near closing time for the bank, no one suspicious had come in or out of the bank, so Kara decided she would check on something, alone, so as not to create any problems. She went directly to the bank and entered. The guys looked on, but didn't like being left behind. Approximately fifteen minutes went by, and then Kara exited the bank and walked across the street to get into the car. Matt says, "Well, what's going on?" She replies, "Our person, whatever her name is, ditched the purse into a safety deposit box. I asked the receptionist if Miss Monahyn was available. The receptionist looked kind of strange and said no one by that name was in the bank. So, I told her I had noticed her come in a few minutes ago and wandered if she were still here. She said no one was in the bank, except employees, and the last customer, a young lady did not go by that name. I asked what name she went by, but she said she couldn't say. So, unless one of you have a lot of pull with the banker, we are just about sunk. I'd bet the phone number is as phony as the name, she gave." Bruce spoke up, "What do you think? She was paid, right, by the killer. If we could catch up to her, she might lead us to the real killer." Kara says, "Yes, maybe, but we don't have anything to help us find her, nothing. But, we know where the purse is, and I bet if we tell the Chief, he could get a search warrant to see whose name the locker is in." Matt says, "That takes time, do we really want to go down that path?" "It's all we have right now, and besides we're closer to finding the killer, now, than we have ever been. At least we know the purse is involved with the case." Says Kara.

Their next move, then, was to go to the Chief and tell him of the clutch, the young lady, and how it happened to be in a locker at the bank, and finally, how they have to rely on the police to find who has the locker and retrieve the evidence. So, this is what happened in the hours of the next day. At the station, the Chief says, "Why didn't you come to me sooner with this, so I could have picked her up, after she left the bank?" Kara responds, "She lied, and now we need to know who she lied for." After this, the Chief decided to get the warrant that day, so as not to waste any time. The Chief had to call the President of the Bank at home, since it was a Saturday and no time was to be lost. At the bank, the President of the Bank immediately went to the the register of listings for the lockboxes and found the number associated with the box with the purse. They looked inside and found that the box was empty. Kara swiftly states, "This is not right, something is wrong." The Chief says, "There sure is, where, is this, so called, purse?" Kara again says, "We had a tiny transmitter put in the lining of the purse, and it led us here where the phony came. Let me see if the transmitter is still operational." She pulled out her phone, where the App. was, and swiped it. The indicator showed the transmitter to be in the bank in a different box. The Chief told the banker to open it, which he proceeded to do, and there was the purse. "I want to know whose lock box this belongs to, now!" Exclaimed the Chief. The banker went to the register and brought it to the Chief and spoke out the name, "Elizabeth Reeves." Stunned and perplexed, the Chief and everyone left the bank. The Chief now had the evidence, he wanted, but the mystery was just as mysterious as before, if not more. That evening, Kara, Bruce, and Matt met at Bruce's office, and they began trying to put this new piece of the puzzle in place. Matt spoke first, "Well, we know that Beth was not going to pick up the purse, so who had a key to her lock box? I don't even have a key to her box. It has to be whoever killed her, and they stole the key at that time." Kara says, "That's one explanation, but it could have been,

Beth trusted someone so much as to give her, or someone, the key for his or her use, when doing transactions
from her shop."

"Who knows? We can only speculate, now, since the
woman who had the key has disappeared." Bruce states.
Kara speaks, "You know, during all the looking and
searching in Beth's shop and during my searches at the
Park, or possibly somewhere else, I noticed, and I only
have a vague memory of a key such as the one used at
the bank. It could be just a coincidence, but I think that
this is not only the key to the box, but this is the key to
unravel the whole mystery. Where ever that key is, we'll
find our killer. I have to think of where, exactly, I saw a
key like that. But, it could be my imagination. I want to get
this solved, so badly, I may have dreamed it. I don't know
right now."

Kara was showing signs of stress at this point, due
to the elusive answer to this mystery, and she finally,
said, "I need to go, I have to put all this out of my mind
for a while. But, tomorrow, I think we need to go over
some of the information Bruce gathered, regarding the
people at the Emporium. They're still a pretty suspicious bunch, and who knows, we might stumble onto
something else to help with the case." And with that
said, she left to go home.

The next few days were of not much significance. Kara
had gone back to work, and Bruce was busy with work and
still checking into the people at the Emporium collectibles
shop. While in a slow time at work, he was looking over
the information he had gotten on the people at the shop,
and he compared this with the other information retrieved

earlier by the group. He found the name of someone who hadn't been noted before. A secretary at the shop had not been discovered. Assuming he would get more information from her, rather than any of the shop owners or others connected with the business, he decided to find a phone number for her and call, after all nothing ventured, nothing gained. After searching on the computer, he found her number and took a moment to dial the number. "Hello" said the female voice at the other end. Bruce spoke softly, as not to offend "Yes, Miss Sanders, my name is Bruce Stanton, and I'm a real estate broker, and I need to ask a few questions for a transaction I'm involved with. Would you mind if I ask you something?" "I don't know of any real estate, but you can ask." She says. "I see here that your shop's name came up as a financial reference as to doing business with another collectable shop in Rossville. What I need is does your company's people do work with anyone like this in Rossville?" asked Bruce. "Well, I don't know, I may not be supposed to let out such information. But, I can tell you that we have conducted business with a person named Reeves within the past four months. I see we have had two appointments in Rossville in that time period, but I'm afraid to say any more due to I could lose my job. So, I believe I'm done." She replied. With that, she hangs up. Bruce wasn't surprised, and after all he had gotten some new information. He thought he should tell Kara immediately, so he called to say "Of the new information on our friends at the Emporium, I've found something very interesting." And, he went on to tell her of what had just transpired. Both thought this was a clue that had to be followed up on, so Kara told Matt, and they decided to all go to Chaffee and have a little talk with these people the very next day.

The next day at the Emporium, the three had no plan and had only their wits to guide them in their quest to find the truth. They walked in as if they owned the shop and asked the man behind the counter if he was the owner. He went back behind a wall and out came a woman of about fifty seven years old with graying hair and a foreign descent. It was Bruce who said, "Ma'am, you may not remember us, but we were here before about a certain coin, but that's not why we're here now. I'll get right to the point. This is Matt Reeves, and I believe you had a couple of appointments with his deceased wife, Beth Reeves, some time ago, and we believe you know something about the death of his wife. Before, we call the police, we will give you the chance to tell us what you know, or else." She retorted, "You have no right to come in here like this and make demands." Kara speaks up, "Oh, but, we do, since Matt here is looking for his wife's killer, and your company's name has come up more than once. We know you stole that rare coin, that the police have now, and they know it too! It's just a matter of time before you will be carted off for poor Beth's murder, unless you talk to us, now." The woman thought for a minute, then bowed her head and sighed, saying, "It's true, we had some appointments with the owner of an export shop, named Reeves, but that is all. We were to purchase the coin, you speak of, and we were to meet at the Park in Rossville, and we did go to the Park, but we found her dead. We became worried that we would be blamed, and we left without the coin or ever talking to her that day."

The three friends paused a moment, then Matt says, "Did you see how she died? Did she show as if in pain?" Kara speaks, "Did you see anything at all, anything we could use to find the real killer, providing your story is true?" The woman replies, "It is the truth, and no we didn't stay around long enough to look at anything, because we heard a noise behind us in the nearby bushes, and we hurried away as soon as we could." The three looked at each other and they then decided whoever was in the bushes must have been the real killer.

Upon leaving the shop, they stopped to get drinks at a nearby drive through restaurant. It was Bruce who said, "I believe that woman, and I believe we just eliminated a suspect. What next?" Kara replied, "I don't know. If the Chief doesn't find that young lady, or the person using the box in Beth's name, I'm afraid we are at an impasse. Sure, someone hired her, and she may be able to tell us something about who hired her, if the Chief finds her, that is." "Any way you look at it, there's not much we can do at the moment, is there?" asked Bruce. They all shook their heads in agreement and headed back to Rossville.

They had decided to table any further action on the matter until something else turned up, or the clues, they already had, led them somewhere else.

The next day led Kara and Matt to the Library and Bruce to the realty office. They felt the best thing to do was get to work, and their stress factors would be lower by not thinking about the case. After a few hours of work, Kara found herself talking with Matt and Ms. Abbott at the break room during break. Matt suggested, "We need to work something out to let Ms. Abbott off a couple of days, since she has been carrying the load, while we were out. Do you agree, Kara?" An immediate reply of, "Yes, and it should be paid time off." Ms. Abbott smiled and said, "Oh, that's not necessary. Actually, I live alone, and work is more to my liking, than sitting around doing nothing. You know what I mean, don't you? I've worked here with Mr. Reeves for a long time, and I love it here, and I love him. He's a wonderful employer and leader." Matt spoke up, "I didn't know you were so endearing toward me. I really am quite fond of you, too. You've been a great asset and a wonderful co-worker."

At the end of the day, Kara approached Matt and asked if he and Bruce would like to eat dinner at her place that evening. Matt asked, "What's the occasion?" Kara replied, "Nothing, except I do need to say something to you and Bruce. It's something that has just come up."

At dinner that evening, the three sat down just after eating, and Kara went to her safe place, where the clues were stored and brought everything out in the open and sprawled out on the floor. They had only copies or photos of some things, such as the coin, the candy wrapper, the lipstick tube (believed to be Beth's), the purse, the diary, the books, Kara had checked out, one about poisons and one about a Black Widow killer, and now, the photo of the lockbox key. She points to all these items or photos of some of these items, and says, " I've gone over these so many times, I don't need to look at them anymore, I know them from memory. Some you may not be familiar with, due to my outside reading and some outside investigation. I've said for some time now, the puzzle is almost complete with a couple of missing pieces. Well, I believe the missing pieces are obvious to me, now. So, I want you both to be at the Library tomorrow morning at nine o'clock, and I'll show you what I mean. Agreed?"

The next morning, Kara was at the Library early, before opening, before anyone was there. She had something she needed to look at. She saw what she wanted to see, and she walked over to the doors of the building and opened them. Within a few minutes, Matt was there and a few minutes after that, Ms. Abbott came in. It was approaching opening time of nine o'clock, when Bruce came up to the door to enter and sauntered in. Kara, with a certain directness, said to everyone, "Please follow me. I believe you'll find this very interesting." She then went to the front desk and laid all the photos and any copies of clues on the desk, saying, "This is the investigation regarding Beth's demise. Notice there is no suspect in this array of clues. That is because the suspects were many, but all were eliminated by common sense or by the process of elimination. Some didn't have the motive, some didn't have the means, some didn't have the potential, and some didn't have the gumption. Anyhow, we are here today to let it be known, the killer had to be one of two people. It was to be either the lockbox owner who had the key and left instructions for everything after her demise." Matt interrupted, "Are you saying Beth killed herself? Impossible! How could she have done such a thing?"

"She may have had it all planned with a different method, of that I'm not entirely certain, but everything still points to her, except, there was one who realized what was happening. The one who dropped her purse when escaping. Her name was on the purse, even if she was intended to be only an observer in the first of the scenario. Isn't that right Abby?" She said as she turned to Ms. Abbott. Kara continued, "The innocent elderly, librarian, no one would suspect, am I correct?" Ms. Abbott fidgety and sort of stunned, said, "Yes, I followed Mrs. Reeves' movements for a long time, years to be exact, and I saw what she was doing to Mr. Reeves, her affairs and such, made him talked about, and not in a good way, with all the rumors. And, during the time I had watched her, I found out she was going to kill herself, after I read some of her instructions to her attorney. He was to tell after she was gone, how she was full of remorse and couldn't live with herself. But, then I noticed her one evening at her shop, when she didn't know I was watching, where she put her special books, her accounts and diaries. She said on one page, her last entry, "she just couldn't do it", and then tore out the page. That's when I saw it in the waste basket. Anyhow, she had gone this far. I couldn't bear thinking Mr. Reeves would have to keep up the life she was making for him. I couldn't have that. I did some research on poison, and I was able to make some odorless, tasteless concentrate and apply it to her lipstick, the one Mr. Reeves bought for her. It seemed fitting. I slipped it back in her purse that evening, and followed her to the Park, where she was to meet someone. Well, I watched from the bushes and saw her use the lipstick for the last time. I would have taken the tube, but the people she was meeting came and realized she was dead. I accidentally, dropped my clutch, the one my niece gave me. She always called me Abby. This scared off the people who were in awe, and I got scared also, and ran away, leaving her purse and her things scattered all round, along with my clutch. I suppose you found the lockbox key in my desk. Is that true?" As she looked at Kara. Kara nodded and said, "I notified the police to be here at nine thirty. They will be here soon. Is there anything you need of us? I hate that it was true." Just then, the police Chief rushed in and looked at everyone and said, "Which one of you did it?" He then took Ms. Abbott out to the car and drove away.

THE END

Bob R Creel